MISTLETOE SUMMER

APPLEBOTTOM MATCHMAKER SOCIETY

ABBY TYLER

SUMMARY

It was love at first sight. For their dogs.

Cody Jones didn't expect to ever return to Applebottom, planning a long life of military service and world travel.

But a devastating injury in Iraq narrows his options.

In walks Melody Hopkins and her puppy dog Mistletoe. His service dog Tyrus can't seem to live without the fluff ball. What's a veteran and dog dad to do?

AbbyTyler
PO Box 160116
Austin, TX 78716
www.abbytyler.com

Paperback ISBN: 9781938150890

Edition 1.o

MEETING MINUTES

APPLEBOTTOM TOWN SQUARE PROPRIETORS
Gertrude Vogel, secretary
Because nobody else knows how to hold a pen anymore.

Today, before we even got the coffee poured, Delilah Jones, owner of Nothing But a Pound Dog, burst out that her son Cody was coming back from his military service.

The shop owners erupted with enthusiasm about his return.

"How bad is it?" I asked, and pretty much everybody turned to give me the evil eye.

Delilah gripped her coffee like it was the last Tickle Me Elmo at Walmart. "He walks with a limp, so don't be surprised when you see that. The PTSD is still there. Probably always will be. He has a therapy dog named Tyrus."

She looked down into her mug. "I'm just glad he's finally coming home."

Ol' softhearted Maude Lewis, co-owner of our pie shop, reached over and gave Delilah's arm a little pat. "I know you'll take good care of him, Delilah. What can we do to help?"

She laughed a little. "I don't think he needs to be matched with anybody. Not right now. But I've been trying to come up with something he can do in town."

Mayor T-bone spoke up next. "Nothing will eat away at a man more than having nothing to do but think about his problems."

We all turned to T-bone at that nugget of insight. He wasn't known for his good advice, being half hermit, half Hell's Angel.

"I agree," Delilah said. "And I've been thinking."

"Everybody hold onto your coffee mugs," I said, and Maude gave me a *Can it, Gertrude* look that I've been familiar with for thirty years.

Delilah tried again. "I've been meaning to expand the bakery. McIntyre's old hardware store has been closed down for coming on ten years, but his son never did anything with it."

"That old storefront is an eyesore," I said. And it was, the blacked-out windows staring onto Town Square like something dead.

"Exactly," Delilah said. "And it shares a wall with my bakery."

"Did Kyle sell it to you?" asked Danny Cole-Smith, the co-owner of Applebottom Blossoms.

"No, I couldn't afford that," Delilah said. "He's agreed to lease it to me."

"You're going to need some help," T-bone said. "That store is a disaster inside."

"I know," Delilah said. "But I thought that's where Cody could come in. He's perfectly able to move things around, clean up, and repair stuff. He got a lot of experience in the Army."

Everyone generally agreed that this was a good call.

"What will you put in there?" Maude asked.

"I wanted to expand the toy wall I already have in the bakery. Start selling regular dog food and cat things. Maybe get some fish."

"Well, that sounds perfectly grand," Maude said. "I can't wait to see what you and Cody do with it. Is he going to run it?"

"If he wants to," Delilah said. "I'm not sure we can think that far ahead."

Another general murmur of agreement.

"I suppose we can table any matchmaking for another day," Betty Johnson said. She owned Tea for Two and was singlehandedly trying to match up all the singles in town, whether they liked it or not.

Maude unveiled our pie for the upcoming summer, a sweet strawberry-rhubarb. And that shut up everybody's gabbing.

Meeting adjourned.

CHAPTER 1

*M*elody Hopkins was too broke to buy a dog biscuit.

Her dog Mistletoe's nose twitched as they rounded the corner of Town Square near the doggy bakery. When they reached the door, the sandy-brown Pomeranian sat her rump on the ground, refusing to move.

"Sorry, Mistletoe," Melody said. "I just can't."

The fluffy dog looked up at her with pleading eyes. They'd spent ten years together. Mistletoe had been there for everything. Melody's first date. First prom. Graduation. They had parted briefly for a year when Melody lived in the dorms, but were triumphantly reunited when she rented a house with three other girls.

And now they were in Applebottom. Melody had survived two years as a math teacher and pep squad coach. And she loved her job, even if it wasn't the highest paying gig.

But Mistletoe definitely liked fancy things.

Like two-dollar, hand-made dog biscuits.

"I don't have the money right now," she said to the pup.

To Melody's complete embarrassment, the door opened, and Delilah herself caught the last few words.

"Nonsense," she said. "I've got lovely free samples right inside. Come on in."

Mistletoe darted inside the shop, pulling Melody along, her face blossoming hot. She didn't like to admit her situation to anyone.

But Delilah did, in fact, have a big tray of broken up dog cookies sitting on the counter. Delilah scooped up a handful and leaned down with one for Mistletoe.

"Say '*please*,'" Delilah said.

Mistletoe gave a sharp bark.

"Such a good girl!"

If anyone was to learn about Melody's situation, at least it was Delilah. Melody adored her. Delilah knew all the pups of Applebottom and loved them as much as their owners did. Mistletoe gulped down her cookie, and Delilah passed the rest to Melody. "For Mom to dole out," she told her. "You ready for summer?"

"We are," Melody said. "The last day of school can't get here fast enough."

"Just one week, right?"

"Yes!"

In the next store over, a great thud broke the quiet, then a string of muffled words, none of them friendly.

"Is somebody opening the old shop next door?" Melody asked.

Delilah stood up straight, pulling on the hem of her

oversized T-shirt. It read, "My Other Kid is a Dog" in sparkling letters.

"Actually, I'm expanding Nothing But a Pound Dog to be a full-fledged pet store." She gestured to a rectangle taped onto the wall beside her. "Going to open a walk-through right there once the dust settles next door."

"Can I see?" Melody asked.

Delilah glanced around. The shop was empty, other than her bulldog Bruno snoozing in an open crate behind the counter.

"Sure, why not?"

They headed out the door and down to the next storefront. The windows had been painted black as long as Melody had lived in town.

"Are you excited to expand?" she asked.

"I am," Delilah said. "I won't duplicate what the local grocery store has, but cater to people who want fancier things."

Melody glanced down at Mistletoe. She definitely wanted those things for her pup, but she just couldn't manage. At least not right now.

Mistletoe seemed to have forgotten the cookies as she trotted along the sidewalk, so Melody shoved them in the pocket of her shorts.

A rag stuffed in the door kept it open a crack. A small sign taped to the outside read, "Help Wanted."

"Are you already hiring people to run the shop?" Melody asked as Delilah pulled out the rag and opened the door.

"No. My son Cody will probably help me out. I need

3

someone for the interior painting. I had hoped old Jeb would be able to fit me in, but he's got some big construction job and his whole crew is tied up."

They went inside. Mistletoe almost balked, the air was so full of dust. The lights were yellow and dim, and half of them were out. The blacked-out windows cut off any natural light.

"I really need to climb up there and replace the bulbs," Delilah said. "Maybe I'll get my husband to do it."

"It'll be better when the windows are clear again."

"Yes. I need to hire someone to scrape them."

"Cody can't do that?"

"He doesn't climb ladders."

She didn't elaborate, so Melody didn't ask.

But this gave her an idea.

"Are you looking for a professional person to paint and scrape?"

"Not really. Anybody who's good with a brush. My main concern is the height." She hesitated. "Cody only works from the ground."

"I could do the high parts. I stand on ladders every day to keep the pep squad organized. And I have zero fear of heights. I was always the girl they threw in the air."

Delilah brushed aside a cobweb that stretched from a light fixture to the wall. "Right. You were a cheerleader in college, weren't you?"

"I was." If only that had translated into a career. She'd tried out for several pro teams after graduation, but it turned out she hadn't been *that* good.

"Cody!" Delilah called. "You back there?"

A figure filled the doorway at the rear of the shop. Melody couldn't really make him out at first, as he was mostly in silhouette.

But he was tall with broad shoulders, she could see that much.

Her heart sped up a little, wondering if he was single. One of the hardest things about living in a small town was how few eligible men were around. She hadn't gone out with anyone since she'd arrived two years ago.

Cody didn't walk out into the room. "Who's that?" he asked. His voice was rough. He seemed to be annoyed that they had interrupted him.

"Melody Hopkins," Delilah said. "She teaches at the high school. Sounds like she's going to help paint." She turned to Melody. "Are you serious about working?"

"Definitely," she said, already spinning figures in her mind, hourly wages and how long the job would take. "Summer vacation starts in a week, but I could come sooner if you need, after school."

"Why don't you come by tomorrow to go over things? Cody can get the paint and supplies in order."

Cody coughed from his position at the back door. "You never said I would have company."

His voice could have curdled milk. Clearly, he didn't want anybody around.

But Melody wasn't a pep squad leader and former cheerleader for nothing.

She wrapped Mistletoe's leash around her wrist and strode right through the empty room.

She extended her free hand. "I'm Melody. I've lived

here in Applebottom almost two years now. I'm so glad to meet you, and I think we will work together just great."

He shook her hand only for a moment before dropping it like he'd been burned. Now that she was closer, she took in his wild brown hair and the rough stubble across his jaw. He wore a black T-shirt. He was handsome in a dark, brooding sort of way.

His eyes met hers, and she swallowed involuntarily. He wasn't happy. That was clear.

"I prefer to work alone," he said.

Delilah let out a nervous laugh. "Oh, Cody, it will be all right."

"I didn't agree to work with anybody. Especially not a Manic Pixie Dream Girl."

Melody kept her smile firmly in place. It wasn't the first time someone had judged her for being too cute, too perky, and too positive. People equated it with being empty-headed, silly, and ridiculous.

"Well," she said, "*this* Manic Pixie Dream Girl happens to teach calculus."

An eyebrow did lift at that, but his overall expression remained menacing and definitely unwelcome.

He turned to his mother. "I don't need help."

Mistletoe let out an excited bark. She lunged forward, straight for Cody.

"No, baby," Melody called. Dang it, the last thing she needed was for her dog to jump all over him right now.

But Mistletoe ignored her, straining at the end of her leash.

Cody looked down at the little dog in annoyance.

"I'm so sorry," Melody said.

A low shadow appeared behind him, then a long, furry snout poked out beside his leg.

A golden retriever.

"Who's this?" Melody asked, crouching down to get a closer look.

"Tyrus," Cody said, almost as if he didn't want to share his name with her. But then he kneeled next to his dog, and his tone completely changed. "Be a good dog, now. We have visitors."

Interesting. Cody's voice lost all its harshness when he spoke to the dog. His long fingers trailed through the retriever's silky fur.

Mistletoe strained forward, her quivering nose finally touching Tyrus's face.

Tyrus stepped forward, and the two of them sniffed each other. Melody spotted a red *Service Dog* vest. She swallowed again. What was it for?

"Come on, Mistletoe," Melody said. "Let Cody and Tyrus do their work."

But the two dogs would have nothing of it. Mistletoe fit herself under Tyrus's neck, and the bigger dog stood over her in a protective stance.

Melody tried to reel in the leash, but each time Mistletoe was forced to take a step away, Tyrus moved forward to maintain their position.

"I guess they like each other," she said.

"Figures," Cody said. The menacing tone had returned.

"Come on, Mistletoe," Melody said, finally reaching

down to pull the fluffy dog away from the retriever. She held the unhappy dog against her chest.

"That's enough, Tyrus," Cody said. "Come on back."

With great reluctance, Tyrus returned to Cody's side.

Mistletoe tried to scramble back down, but Melody pinned her with one arm and dug a cookie out of her pocket.

"Looks like they've become fast friends," Delilah said.

Melody let out a nervous laugh. "I've never seen her bond with another dog like this before."

"Me neither," Cody said. "Tyrus is a trained therapy dog. He's not supposed to get distracted while he's on duty."

Mistletoe ignored the cookie and let out a low whine, begging to be put back down. It was breaking Melody's heart. "Come on, baby girl," she said. "Eat a cookie."

Tyrus let out a low, quiet bark.

Cody kneeled next to him, his shirt straining over his muscled shoulders. Melody had to drag her gaze away.

"What's gotten into you, Tyrus? You forget your training?" He looked over at the squirming Pomeranian with an expression of suspicion.

Delilah turned to Melody. "So you can come by tomorrow for instructions? I'm afraid I won't have much time to get away once summer begins. It'll be busy, and I will have my grandson a lot."

"Absolutely. And you won't have to worry about

watching over me. I'm a self-starter."

Cody looked up from where his hand gripped Tyrus's collar. "Sounds like I don't have a say in the matter," he said.

"It's just until the painting is done," Delilah said. "You two will like each other. I'm sure of it."

Melody's belly quaked, but she still extended her hand to Cody again. "I look forward to it."

This time, he didn't jerk away the moment they came in contact. His hand was warm and strong, his fingers wrapping around her palm. Her heart pattered unevenly, even though he had been a bit of a brute. He was nice to his dog, so he did have it in him. He just liked to work alone. She understood. She'd stay out of his way until she figured out if they could be friends.

Mistletoe squirmed, and Melody let Cody go so she could manage the pup with both hands. Her eyes caught Cody's, and she swore she saw something else there now. Amusement? Maybe it was about the dogs.

She headed for the door and didn't set Mistletoe down until they were outside. The sun streamed down like it was telling her life was about to get grand.

Something had changed today, as if the world had tilted in her direction. She'd found a way to earn a little more pocket money to get her out of the hole she was in.

And she'd met a man. A strong, gruff, intriguing man who loved his dog.

She reached out with her finger, as if her list of *Best Qualities* was hovering in the air in front of her.

And she checked off the very first box.

CHAPTER 2

*W*hen both the girl and his mother had finally gone, Cody hobbled over to the stepladder with a seat on top and lowered himself down. When he'd heard the higher, younger voice come in the front of the store, he hadn't wanted to use his walking cane.

This, of course, was pure foolishness. The moment he'd seen the woman, her long waves of dark hair, bright smile, and perfect everything, he knew there was no way someone like her would ever be interested in a washed-up, small-town, broken-down war veteran who couldn't even walk straight.

Tyrus sat close to him. His long golden tail wagged happily, but Cody could see in his eyes that he was feeling concerned.

"It's all right," he told him. "At least *you* made a good impression."

Tyrus nudged his nose beneath Cody's hand, and

Cody began to pet him absently. Cody sat there a while, stroking the dog's soft head until his body relaxed.

Whenever he felt any sort of threat, even if it was just a cute girl, the part of his brain that controlled his fear response jumped into the red zone. He became this angry, rough robot-man who responded in ways that made Cody disgusted with himself. He still wasn't completely able to control it.

Cody's therapist back at the VA hospital, when they were still trying to untangle his overreactions, said that when he was under stress, he subconsciously emulated someone he thought was stronger than him.

Cody knew it was Sergeant Black, who'd gotten him through basic training. He could hear it in how he'd spit out his words like they were cut with a saw. Perfect for military work. Civilian, not so much.

It made sense that he'd mimic someone fierce to get him through a tough spot, although not much about his condition was logical otherwise. He'd been through all sorts of treatments. There was one where they tracked his eyes while they asked him questions. Another where they attached a gadget to his finger to measure his respiration and heart rate. He'd had to breathe in and out to the rhythm of a circle growing and shrinking on a screen.

He'd been in small groups and big groups. Done more solo therapy sessions than he could count.

And he was better. For the most part, he could control the worst of the violent outbursts. He no longer picked up objects and hurled them without any consideration as to what they were or who might be in the way.

And about ninety percent of the time, he could control himself from yelling out loud, even when the noises in his head were so overwhelming, he felt as though he had to rise to meet them or they would bury him like a pile of rocks.

He'd tried the pills, too. Four different kinds. They had helped when things were at their worst, but as he got better, he'd wanted to shake the fogginess they gave him, the sense that he wasn't quite alive.

They'd finally sent them home, but the damage remained. Not just to his leg. But his head. He no longer had a certainty that his body would respond in the ways he told it to.

He didn't know what to do with himself. He couldn't do missions anymore, and he knew that. While his limp would get better in time, his leg was never going to work perfectly.

And his technical expertise was pretty specific. Combat vehicles. Classified military technology. Some of it applied to general electronics or mechanical work, but most of it couldn't.

He wasn't sure he wanted to run a pet store, but his mother had overcommitted herself on this project, and he would help her out until he figured out what he wanted to do.

His thoughts drifted to the girl again. Melody. He'd never seen anyone quite like her. That probably wasn't true, maybe on movie screens. But certainly not up close.

She had a bright cheerfulness about her that made him irritable. He couldn't match it. About the only thing he could do was to wreck it, upset her until she approached him with caution or straight-up disgust.

It would happen. She would arrive full of sunshine, and he'd dim her light until her attitude was as dark as his.

His hand tightened into a fist. Tyrus immediately responded by putting a paw on his knee and letting out a low whine.

"Okay, Tyrus. I hear you. I'm in a thought spiral."

He'd learned about those. The feedback loops inside his head that would eventually cause his amygdala to activate, and his thinking brain to shut down. That was the beauty of his PTSD. He didn't even need fireworks or loud noises or outside triggers to make it come. He could think himself into oblivion.

That was what Tyrus was for. He knew when Cody was in a spiral, and he broke it by forcing Cody to pet him, or distracting him out of his internal thoughts. He'd be lost without the dog, and only because the two of them worked so well together had he been discharged at all.

Cody plunked his feet on the floor and stood up. "Those baseboards aren't going to remove themselves," he said to Tyrus.

He hobbled over to his walking stick and returned to the toolbox he'd been sorting through when his mother had interrupted. He found a hammer and a wedge he could use to separate the boards from the walls. It was simple work, mindless, and low to the ground.

This, at least, he could do.

And next time he saw Melody, he'd do better.

CHAPTER 3

On Sunday morning, Melody felt her nerves jangling throughout her body as she walked from her little rented house to Town Square.

She knew she was a people pleaser. She felt uncomfortable when people disliked her, and she tried hard to be kind to everyone.

Not that she was "Miss Perfect" or some Pollyanna. She just liked people, even grumpy ones like Cody, and she wanted them to like her back.

When she arrived at the black-painted windows, she was surprised to find the front door locked.

Was she early? She didn't think so. She'd actually been running a little late.

She pulled her phone out of her back pocket and confirmed that she was indeed about three minutes late. She walked along the windows, but there weren't any scratches in the dark surface big enough to peek through.

She moved down to Nothing But a Pound Dog, but

the bakery was also locked up tight. That was to be expected. It didn't open until noon on Sundays. That was an hour away.

So what should she do now? Wait? All the stores of Town Square were closed at this hour. She was about to leave when she noticed a light click on, brightening the unpainted inch or so at the top of the windows.

Someone was in there.

The door was still locked, so she knocked on it.

For a long moment, there was nothing. Then she made out a quiet *thump-thump-thump.* As she waited, it grew a little louder. Melody's nerves hit a peak. What was going on?

She almost backed away, but froze in fear when the lock began to squeak from the inside. At last, the door opened with a sharp tug.

Cody's face appeared in the crack. "You came," he said gruffly. He swung the door wide.

"I did," Melody stammered. "I was just beginning to think I had gotten the time wrong."

Cody moved aside to let her in. Tyrus sat next to him, his long nose tilting as he took her in.

"Good morning, Tyrus!" she said, leaning down to pet his silky ears. The dog was a relief, something easy when Cody was hard. "You're such a beauty."

Tyrus gave her a soft *woof* in response.

She stood up, her nose tingling. The room smelled strongly of fresh paint. Cody must have started the work.

Melody began to worry that they wouldn't need her after all. If Cody did all the painting before school let out just to keep her from coming, she'd be out the extra money she was hoping for.

"You got started," she said, looking around. A fresh coat of paint covered one wall from the floor to about two-thirds of the way up.

She turned to face him. "You made a lot of progress and—"

She halted. Cody stood in the light of the door, wearing dressy clothes and resting heavily on a shiny black cane.

He hadn't had that yesterday.

Her eyes dropped down to it, then immediately bounced back up so she wouldn't make him feel self-conscious.

Now everything became clear. Delilah needed someone to get the high parts because Cody couldn't. Something had happened to his leg. He probably couldn't climb ladders or stand on scaffolds.

"It looks great," she finished, hoping her hesitation wouldn't upset him. "So is it going to be all white inside?"

Cody closed the door with a shove.

"No. You'll be taping off a line about three feet from the ceiling. It will be white up to that point, and red above it, to match the logo."

His words tumbled out like boulders rolling down a hill, rumbling and full of threat. He'd seen her notice the cane. His words were like a dare for her to mention it.

"That sounds pretty," she said. She had no idea how to cover her gaffe. It was no big deal that he walked with the cane. In fact, it was rather distinguished.

But she wouldn't say so. Clearly, it was a sore subject.

"Mom will be here soon," he said. "She got stuck at some church thing for a few extra minutes."

Melody turned away. "Okay. That's fine. I'm not on any sort of schedule."

She pretended to be grossly interested in the newly painted wall. The silence stretched between them.

Cody didn't move from his spot by the door. Melody wondered if he had a problem with her watching him walk. She remembered the *thump-thump* she'd heard approaching while she waited and had a feeling he was self-conscious about it.

She'd encountered people like Cody before, of course. She always tried her best to stay cheerful around them, even if they gave her nothing but nastiness in return.

She'd give this a shot. Sometimes it was best to just get the problem out in the open.

"I know you'd rather work alone," she said. "You said as much yesterday. But I really need the money. Like really, *really* need it. Delilah advertising for help that I can actually do was, like, the biggest lucky break I've gotten in a while."

Cody's foot shuffled a bit, his hand gripping the walking stick. "I see," he said. "Well, I suppose we can work around each other."

Melody let out her breath with a rush. Her eagerness flooded right back, which she knew was one of her superpowers.

"Great," she said. "So, this is just a big empty space

right now. I guess we'll be painting the walls, then putting up shelving of some sort? Maybe the hooks like she has on her accessory wall in the bakery?" She looked around.

Before he could answer, she added, "Are we going to paint the little paw prints on the wall like on her logo? I don't think that would be too hard. The pep squad has been able to replicate any mascot's prints for their signs. It should be easy to make a cardboard stencil and paint inside it."

She knew she was talking breathlessly and a little too fast, but she was so relieved that this was going to work out that she wanted to cry.

"You going to let me get a word in edgewise?" he asked, but she swore he cracked a smile. A smile!

"Probably not," she said. "If I talk too much or too fast, just wave at me or something."

"Should we have a signal?" he asked.

Was he teasing her? Her heart leaped.

"Sure, but make it really obvious," she said. "I *am* only a cheerleader." She twisted the end of her ponytail around her finger and batted her eyelashes like every stereotypical airhead in a comedy movie.

"A cheerleader who teaches calculus," he said.

Her belly flipped that he remembered.

"I like to be unpredictable."

He grunted at that. "The painting has to be done before we can move on with shelving or counters. I'm constructing some things in the back. This place got gutted. It's a lot to do."

"When are you going to open?"

"We're aiming for mid-July."

Melody began to wander the perimeter of the room, pausing to examine paintbrushes and plastic floor covering. "So Delilah is your mom," she said.

"All my life," Cody said, the teasing note returning to his voice.

Melody realized they'd gotten past the hard part. She'd seen his cane, and she hadn't made a big deal about it. That mattered to him.

"I mean, she's your mom, but you haven't lived here in a while. I've been here almost two years. Where have you been?"

Cody's dark tone returned. "A mental hospital."

Melody forced herself to keep walking in the same easy stride. He was trying to shock her. Scare her, maybe.

She wasn't going to let him win.

"How interesting. Patient or doctor?"

He responded with a grunt of laughter.

Look at her go. She'd made him laugh.

"Most definitely a patient," he said.

"Are you doing better now?"

Her voice stayed steady, but her mind was a whirl. Had he hurt somebody? Himself? Was he really sick? Should she be alone with him?

She couldn't stop the flow of thoughts. But then she remembered his dog. They wouldn't issue him a dog and send him home if he was a danger. Her stomach settled.

"Well enough to leave," he said, his voice not quite as gruff.

"Well, I'm glad you're here. How long have you had Tyrus?"

"About four months."

"He's obviously very devoted." She'd made almost a full circle of the room and stood only a few feet from him now. She glanced down at his cane. "Nice stick," she said, then her face flushed as she realized she'd made a double entendre. She pressed her palms to her hot cheeks

But Cody surprised her. "What? This old thing?" He swung it in a circle like he was about to do a dance.

He'd made a joke to alleviate her embarrassment. Her relief was so great that there was a kinder, gentler side to Cody that she burst into suppressed giggles.

"You're funny," she said. "I love a guy who makes me laugh."

For a moment, his expression lightened, as if they were having the easy banter you might expect from two young people. But then he seemed to catch himself, and his eyebrows drew together. His expression went dark.

"Right. That's me. A barrel of laughs."

Melody held her smile. She relied pretty heavily on her instincts about people. And they were telling her that Cody used to be a really lighthearted guy. Then something had changed him; maybe whatever had caused him to also need a walking stick to get around.

And he still hadn't moved from his position near the door, hadn't taken a single step in any direction, as if he was unwilling to let her see him struggle.

Maybe they should just get that part over with.

"So will you show me around the back?" she asked.

Cody hesitated, initially not moving a muscle or saying a word. Silence lingered, but she held his gaze, refusing to let him off the hook. They had to get past this. Maybe then things would settle down between them.

"All right," he finally said. "But it's pretty much chaos back there."

"Exactly as I would expect, given the makeover we're about to do."

Cody set the walking stick down ahead of him. Then he leaned heavily on it as he took a light step forward.

She watched him for a moment, making it clear that his way of getting around did not alter her opinion of him in any way, and then turned to walk beside him to the back.

It was slow going. But she filled the time with comments about the floor, the concept of the red and white paint. Where they might put some paw prints, and if Delilah wanted anything else painted. Her gift of gab was coming in handy.

Eventually, they made it to the back room. Cody had been right. It was chaos.

Tyrus had gone ahead and waited in the doorway. He watched the two of them for a moment with his warm expressive eyes, and then seemed to make a decision about Cody being in good hands and headed to a large lamb's wool bed in the corner.

Melody considered the dog for a moment. "Do you take him everywhere?"

"Pretty much." His tone wasn't quite as dark as

before, as if he'd gotten the worst of it out and had less to hide.

"He's amazing. He therapied my Mistletoe right into forgetting about two-dollar cookies." Melody bit her lip. She shouldn't say cutting things about the expensive dog treats Cody's mother made. They were paying her to paint.

But Cody moved right past the remark. "I've never seen him act like that before."

"Maybe we'll have to get them together again."

Cody caught her eye, and Melody's chest tightened. He had a way of looking at her that made her breath catch.

"Maybe so."

When the conversation lagged, Melody immediately began organizing all the paint by color, the brushes by size, and created a neat stack of the plastic tarps.

For a little while, Cody just watched her, and then he moved on, pulling plastic wrap off shiny metal shelving. She realized he couldn't hang them until the walls were done.

"Is it going to get you behind schedule if I'm not able to paint for another week?" she asked.

"There's plenty to do."

When he seemed absorbed in the task, Melody watched him from the corner of her eye. He was so interesting. When his features were relaxed, he appeared to be a friendly, ordinary guy. A good-looking one, too. His dark hair fell forward.

The flannel stretched across his shoulders as he

worked. He was definitely fit, even if he did walk with a stick.

He glanced up, and she quickly looked back down, making sure all the cans of white paint were arranged with the label facing out.

She felt his gaze on her, and read the side of the can with fierce concentration.

Tyrus made a little *woof* from his bed, and in the next moment, the back door opened.

Delilah rushed into the room. "Oh my goodness, I am so sorry. I should've realized I could never get away from church by eleven."

She hung her purse on a hook by the door. "Thank you for coming ahead, Cody," she said. "Although, I think the ladies would've preferred you stayed to chat a while."

Cody simply shrugged. He focused on the shelves as intently as Melody had been reading paint cans a moment earlier.

There was definitely tension between mother and son. Melody wondered what Delilah thought about Cody's mental hospital stay, if she was worried. Probably so.

"No Mistletoe?" Delilah asked.

"She's pretty fluffy," Melody said. "I tried to picture what would happen if she got into the paint."

Delilah's laughter peeled through the room. "I can't even imagine. But you know that you're welcome to try. She sure did seem to get along with Tyrus. She was very *Lady* to his *Tramp*."

"Tyrus is not a tramp," Cody grumbled.

"Of course he's not," Delilah said, careful to keep her voice bright. "I just meant they got along so well so quickly."

Delilah glanced around. "My, you jumped right in, didn't you? I thought we would go over my plans, and see what you thought, and maybe come up with an order of things."

The next half hour was much easier, with Delilah walking Melody around the main store. She listened intently to Melody's ideas for the logo and paw prints, clapping her hands with delight.

"It's going to be so grand," she said.

"Are you sure you don't want the door cut out early?" Melody asked. "Otherwise we can't paint that wall until the construction is done."

Delilah turned to the wall. "Good point. Stanley's doing that. I'll ask if he can come out this week before you start painting."

Cody's voice from the door was a growl. "I tried to tell her that."

"You did! And I didn't listen!" Delilah's voice went high-pitched again.

Melody clasped her hands together. This was a little hard to watch. Delilah couldn't seem to do anything right for Cody.

"I look forward to getting started," Melody said. "You think I should come next Saturday and get a jumpstart on the week? Or should I wait until Monday?"

"Whatever works for you," Delilah said. "It's hourly, so you can run those hours whenever you want."

"Great," Melody said. She called back at Cody, "See you soon!"

He gave a little wave, and then resumed removing plastic from shelving with exaggerated jerks.

Melody headed out into the sunshine, a mixture of relief and nervousness fluttering through her. The job would work out. She could put up with Cody, even if his moods shifted faster than the gears of a racecar.

He'd clearly been through a lot. She could make allowances. And truly, he couldn't be any grumpier than a group of teenage girls getting on a bus at six in the morning to travel for a game.

And he was intriguing. Something about his rough exterior made her want to move in a little closer. Maybe she could find a way to peel off a few of those hard layers and find the friendly, funny guy she was pretty sure was underneath.

CHAPTER 4

*C*ody grimaced as he got out of bed. He was tight and sore after actual work, and not just the exercises he'd been prescribed by his physical therapist back in Phoenix.

Cody shoved himself out of bed and hobbled over to the walking stick leaning against a chair by the closet. Mornings were always the worst. The pain was a living thing, pulsing in his leg like an alien lived inside. Later on, as his muscles warmed up and loosened, it would settle down.

At least he wasn't living with his mother, not after all his years in tents and barracks. When he'd returned, he'd only been home a week before he'd started asking around about renting something.

The house he'd found had plenty of space and a great backyard for Tyrus to run around. He'd snapped it up immediately, even though his meager things rattled around in the open spaces.

His mother had not complained one bit about his

decision and had his dad move over his bed and an extra armchair. They'd managed to scrounge up a decent sofa and a dining table from thrift shops to make the place livable.

But as he walked to the bathroom, a splintering pain shot up his leg all the way to his hip, and he collapsed against the wall. He bumped the table next to his bed and the alarm clock and a pile of change crashed to the floor.

The combination of the unexpected pain and the loud sounds set off a panic attack he couldn't control.

His breathing increased. The pain in his leg became searing. He looked down, grimacing at the exposed bone and the skin and muscle peeling away. Blood rushed to the floor, and his fingernails scraped at the wall.

His nose filled with the acrid smell of explosives and detonation. Around him, men shouted for help, and others cried out in pain. He shut his eyes but the visions remained.

He felt stuck inside his skin. Part of him knew it wasn't real, but all his senses insisted that it was. A vehicle skidded to his left, and more shouts preceded the *rat-tat-tat* of weapons discharging. He refused to open his eyes. It would pass. It had to pass.

Something wet against his palm didn't fit the scene. A low whine. A handful of fur.

Cody remembered to breathe and looked down at the floor.

There was no blood. No bone. No smoke or other

people. In fact, there was no sound other than slow wheezy breaths.

It was Tyrus, his golden face looking up at him with concern.

He was back.

Cody returned to his bed and sat down. He opened a drawer in the battered nightstand and pulled out the biofeedback device he'd been issued when he'd left the hospital.

He stuck the device on his finger. The screen lit up, alerting him that his heart rate and oxygen levels were indicating distress. Right. As if he didn't know. A series of circles appeared with a reminder to time his breath with the visual. He breathed in with the expanding circles, then exhaled as they contracted. In the corner of the screen, his heart rate began to tick down. The pain lessened. Tyrus sat down at his feet.

He hated using this thing, resenting the admission that he needed it. But it did help. And right now, no one knew he was using it but him.

When he felt in control again, he shut down the device and shoved it back into the drawer. He picked up the alarm clock and the change.

Time to get on with his day.

Tyrus sat up on his haunches, his eyes keenly on Cody.

"I'm all right." He petted the dog's head. "We should get you something to eat."

CHAPTER 5

*M*elody intended to stay away from the store renovation until summer break began.

But she had been distracted for days. She thought about Cody. His walking stick. His attitude. His broad shoulders.

As she waited for a student to puzzle out a particularly tricky equation for his upcoming final exam, she sat at the student desk, her chin in her hand, and imagined what Cody would look like as they went about the business of painting Delilah's store expansion.

"Ms. Hopkins? *Ms. Hopkins?*"

Melody shook herself out of the vision. "Sorry, Jesse. I was miles away. Did you finish?"

Jesse pointed out where he'd gotten stuck, and Melody reviewed the steps again to show him his mistake.

She glanced around her classroom. Colorful posters full of funny math expressions covered the walls. She'd made many of them herself. High school calculus didn't inspire clever slogans or cute characters like elementary math. But when the teacher was also the pep squad coach, you could be certain there would be a little ingenuity.

Melody liked it in Applebottom. The kids were nice. The families were involved. The percentage of college-bound students was probably a little lower than at other places, but that didn't seem to breed complacency. They just liked to stick around, and most did honest work at blue-collar jobs.

She had no real desire to move on. Other than the husband problem.

Which, of course, turned her mind back to Cody Jones.

Mistletoe led the way as Melody meandered the streets of Applebottom. She told herself she wasn't really heading to Town Square. She was simply following Mistletoe as the Pomeranian sniffed from one side of the street to the other.

Of course, somehow they ended up in sight of the black-painted windows.

She ought to ask Delilah about them. It seemed like the work would go more easily if they could see what they were doing. Perhaps scraping the windows should be one of the first things to do, even if it meant passersby could peek in on them.

Who knew, maybe Delilah wanted things to be a

secret, and the dark windows were a part of that. Still, it couldn't hurt to ask.

Mistletoe sniffed the sidewalk, probably searching for any signs of Tyrus. She must have found something because suddenly she bounced on the end of her leash like a fluffy beach ball.

The door was propped open with a rag again. Delilah must do that to make it easy to pass between the shops until they were connected.

Should she knock on the door? Cody probably wasn't expecting anyone to stop by.

Mistletoe scrabbled her paws at the corner of the door. Melody hesitated. This had been a terrible idea. Her dog would go bonkers and disrupt whatever Cody was working on.

But then she heard the buzz of a saw. It whined for a few seconds, then stopped.

A scratchy voice said, "It's now or never."

Then Cody. "It's been measured about twenty times. We're ready."

So there were other people working today. Bolstered with the knowledge that she wasn't interrupting Cody's solitary work, Melody pushed on the door.

"Hello, hello?"

The interior was significantly brighter today, a semi-circle of shop lamps lighting up the space. All the bulbs and fixtures had been replaced, and the store seemed more personable with that alone.

A man in overalls, wisps of gray hair sticking out in every direction, pressed a long slender saw blade against the wall.

Both he and Cody turned to her as the door widened.

Cody wore jeans and a gray T-shirt this time. He sat on the top of the same stepstool she had seen the other day. His expression might have brightened just a bit when he saw her, but she couldn't be sure.

Wishful thinking.

"About to get loud in here," the man called out.

Melody bent down to call Mistletoe, who was sniffing at the far end of her leash. She wouldn't come, so Melody reeled her in. Tyrus was nowhere in sight.

The whine of the saw started up again. Melody watched in fascination as the man made his way up a pale-red chalk line. He paused at the first turn, pulled out, and went in again. He stopped again at the second corner and tugged the saw away from the wall.

Mistletoe began to shake, so Melody sat on the floor and kept her in her lap.

The man repositioned the saw at the base of the wall. She thought Cody's gaze flicked over to her more than once, but she couldn't be sure. The saw began again. When it had almost reached the top corner, the man motioned for Cody to come forward.

Cody stood and placed his hand on the wall. The saw buzzed to the corner, but it didn't come completely loose. Together, the two men pulled on the cut section to work it free. Dust rained down.

Finally, a corner broke out. Melody expected to see through to Delilah's bakery, but there was just a gap and another wall. The two of them pulled on more of the drywall, yanking it apart until the entire rectangle was in pieces on the floor.

"I'll head to the other side," the man said. He turned to Melody. "You don't know me, but my granddaughter Simone is on your pep squad."

Melody jumped to her feet. "I love Simone. She's graduating in a few days!"

"Aye, she is. I'm Stanley."

They shook hands. Stanley headed for the door. "I'll see you in a minute," he said with a laugh, gesturing toward the wall.

With the room quiet again, Tyrus peeked his head out from the back room. Mistletoe bolted to the end of her leash.

"You decided to check things out?" Melody asked the retriever.

But he was too busy to notice her. He and Mistletoe circled each other, sniffing.

"Come here!" she called, kneeling down to pat the floor. Mistletoe didn't pay her any attention, but Tyrus trotted over. He sat next to Melody, and Mistletoe quickly followed and tucked herself beneath his front legs.

"What is it about these dogs that make them so attached?" Melody asked.

"I don't know," Cody said. "I've been meaning to write his trainer to ask."

Melody stroked both of the dogs' fluffy heads. "Maybe even training can't stand in the way of true love," she said.

Cody crossed his arms at that, his face making clear

that he didn't buy that explanation whatsoever. His T-shirt read, "AC/DC" in big white letters.

"Hey!" She turned from the dogs to point at his shirt. "Do you love AC/DC? Because I know I do."

Cody looked down as if he had forgotten what shirt he'd worn that day.

"Well, yeah. Who wouldn't?"

"Lots of people," Melody said. "My mom was a head cheerleader," she paused when Cody rolled his eyes. "Yes, I know that's a big surprise. She decided to play their song *Jailbreak* over the school intercom on Homecoming her senior year and got suspended."

Cody's expression changed to surprise. "Seriously? For playing a song?"

"Yes. She missed the Homecoming dance. Her last one. All because they felt her music choice was grossly inappropriate."

Cody laughed, and Melody felt triumph again that she had loosened him up.

"Well, the song isn't exactly suggesting school is a paradise."

"I'm pretty sure that was her point," she said.

Cody leaned against the wall. "So your mom was a cheerleader and a rebel."

Melody shrugged. "I guess so. She instilled a love of head-banging music in me. She didn't pursue cheerleading after high school, though. Not many do."

"But you did?"

"Yes. I really loved it. The tumbling. The athleticism. Getting tossed in the air."

Cody perked up at that, so she added, "I was always the little one who did the aerials."

"Did anybody ever drop you on your head?" He said it with such a sly suggestiveness that she had to laugh.

"Probably. Thankfully, it did not hinder my ability to do calculus."

Cody pushed away from the wall and shuffled closer. His walking stick was several feet away by the stepladder.

He sat down on the floor next to Melody and the dogs. "So what's the deal with calculus? Those two things just don't add up."

"I'll admit there are not a lot of cheerleaders who major in math," Melody said. "That's part of why I chose it. I mean, for one, I was good at math. But I like the idea of doing something that breaks stereotypes."

Cody propped his elbows on his knees. Melody felt a little glow all over. This was working. She liked him. He certainly could be all gruff, but if you got past it, he was actually kind of sweet.

The saw started up on the other side of the wall, and dust drifted down as the blade made its way up in a line.

"Do you need to go to the other side to help?" Melody asked.

"Not really," Cody said. "I'm just the eye candy."

He'd made a joke. Melody was so caught off guard that she snort-laughed, something she tried desperately to control. She clapped her hand over her mouth and nose. Mistletoe looked up and gave a little yip.

"Sorry," she said. "It comes out like that sometimes."

But Cody was laughing, too. "That's how I will

always know if you're really laughing and not just faking it."

He was right, of course. The other laughs were nervous, or disguising some other emotion. Snort-laughs were real.

"All right, now that you know my most embar-rassing trait, you have to tell me yours," Melody said.

He didn't answer for a moment, and Melody wanted to smack herself. She was bringing up flaws, and now she'd made him self-conscious.

"Something silly," she added, a tremor in her voice.

"I get it," he said. "I guess my most embarrassing thing used to be my goofy hinged thumbs." He held up his hands, wiggling thumbs that were rather oddly flexi-ble, bent like hooks. "But now..." He gestured down to his leg, which looked perfectly normal in a pair of jeans. "Now it's pretty much everything."

"No," Melody started to say, but the banging on the wall resumed, drowning out her voice. Cody turned away, his expression dark, the easy-going camaraderie lost.

A triangle from the corner of the cut section popped loose, falling into the space between the walls. The ceiling to Delilah's bakery became visible.

Cody stood up, so she did, too, watching the wall cave in, chunks falling into the gap.

The smell of dust gave way to the warm baking smells from the ovens of Delilah's shop.

Stanley's face appeared, then Delilah's behind him. They waved, and Cody and Melody waved back.

"I'll be back over in a sec," Stanley said. "I'm going to clean up this side."

"I guess I should start picking up these," Cody said, limping over to the gap to stack the rough-edged sections of the wall.

"I can help," she said, stepping closer.

But Cody waved her away. "That's all right. We'll have it all clean by the time you're ready to paint."

He was back to cold Cody. Melody reached for Mistletoe's leash to pull her from Tyrus. "See you then," she said.

Cody kept working, his back to her. Melody reeled Mistletoe in and headed back out into the bright afternoon.

Cody was tough. If she wanted anything more than a terse working relationship, she'd have to think before she opened her foolish mouth.

CHAPTER 6

*A*s Cody rolled the dumbbell up from his knee to his shoulder, the old battle drummed inside his head. Ever since he'd met Melody, he'd become increasingly aware of how different he was from the person he'd been when he'd left his small town five years ago.

He wasn't sure he could be anybody to her. He was too broken.

It was Saturday, the first day of summer. He could see Melody today if he wanted. She was getting a head start, not even waiting for Monday.

His mother, with his nephew in tow, was meeting her before the bakery opened to show her where to start painting.

That was two hours away. He'd risen before dawn, unable to sleep, restless and agitated. He was pretty certain he'd had the dreams again, but the medicine suppressed them. He'd awakened unaware of exactly what had occurred while he'd slumbered, left only with the pounding heart, sweaty palms, and a disconnected sense of doom.

So he worked out. He could pummel the demons with a heavy punching bag, and drive them away with dumbbell reps.

He finished his bicep rotation and moved on to legs. He hated the legwork. It was painful and somewhat pointless. His right leg would never be like it was, not even close. A particularly sympathetic physical therapist had extended his treatment well past standard protocol. He knew she'd been buying him time, hoping the other symptoms would settle down while he was focused on healing physically.

She'd been wrong.

He began the leg presses, knowing that his left leg was doing all the work.

He cycled through, then did individual calves. Despite the fact he was alone, removing the pins to change the weights from left to right was embarrassing. A nine-year-old could probably lift more.

He finished the rotation, then did it again. It was the only thing that soothed him.

Finally, Cody glanced at the clock. Half an hour until Melody would be up at the store. He'd told his mother last night that he wasn't sure he'd make it in that early, and she should be there to tell Melody what she wanted.

He'd blamed the early start on his dog. His routine. The things she knew would be a lie but would not question. His mother was intuitive. She'd taken it hard when he hadn't come home for so long. But she accepted him completely. That was something.

He got in the shower, letting the water wash away the negativity. That was a phrase from one of the therapists. Funny how some of them stuck in your mind.

Every day is a new day.

Every journey begins with one step.

You don't know what you're capable of until you try.

The trite expressions rained down on him.

He pictured the words swirling into the drain. He was left with an image of Melody instead. Her hair cascading down her shoulders. The way she clapped her hand over her nose and mouth when she snort-laughed.

That had been funny.

He thought of a new phrase: *A snort-laugh a day keeps the PTSD away.*

He sucked in a laugh, sputtering when warm water shot up his nose.

He coughed and laughed and coughed and laughed, and it felt as though maybe something did happen. Like maybe some of the dozens of knots in his neck and shoulders and back had loosened up just a little.

She was good for him. Light to his dark. He vowed not to snuff her joy, to make her unhappy to see him. So far she'd been resilient, even when he was not his best self.

He'd try.

But he needed to hurry. He should be at the store when Melody got there.

When Cody arrived to unlock the back door of the new expansion, his mother was just pulling up.

"Oh good," she said, opening the car for his sister's son, William.

The boy was only six, and Cody had to admit to not knowing him well. He'd been a baby when Cody left for basic training. And the little bit of time they'd spent together on visits back home hadn't been particularly useful in getting to know the kid. He'd only been old enough to hold a conversation in the last two years, and, of course, Cody had spent them elsewhere.

Still, he gave the friendly uncle role a try. He ruffled the kid's hair and said, "So, Billy, you going to eat some dog treats?"

The boy ducked away from his hand with a laugh. "No way! It's William, not Billy."

"But I like Billy."

"Then I'm going to call you Uncle Toady."

Cody had to laugh at that. The boy was a lot like he'd been as a kid. "I say that's up for negotiation. Would you rather I called you Willy instead?"

"Cody!" his mother sputtered.

Cody laughed. "What? You think two boys don't make inappropriate nicknames for each other?"

His mother shook her head, but a smile flirted with the edges of her mouth.

"Piggyback!" William insisted.

"Oh no," Delilah said quickly. "Not with Uncle Cody. Do that with your dad."

Cody's gut tensed. So he wasn't ever going to be

father material if he couldn't give a kid a piggyback ride?

"I got this, Mom."

He squatted on his good leg and braced himself on the cane. "Hop up, but hold on tight."

His mother pressed her lips together tightly as William made a running jump onto Cody's back. For a moment, he felt the weariness from that morning's workout, and his hand slipped on the stick.

But he righted himself and managed to stand. The boy wrapped his legs around Cody's waist, and Cody took a second to lock them together.

"Hold tight here," Cody said. "Your gimpy old uncle needs one hand free for his cane."

William just laughed. "Mom carries a stick like that when we walk the dog."

The three of them headed toward the back door. "Really?" Cody asked. "Why's that?"

"Officer Stone has a new dog from the shelter, and he's not trained," William said soberly. "Mama said he could attack Frisco." Frisco was his sister's elderly Basset Hound.

Delilah popped the door open. "Oh, I don't think Nero would do that. Savannah and Luke worked with him before he left the shelter."

Cody felt William shrug, his tiny body shifting on Cody's back. "That's just what Mama says."

"Well, my cane is for something special," Cody said. They entered the dark space of the back of the expansion, the smell of paint and dust overwhelming his nose.

"What's that?"

Cody crouched down again and released the boy to the floor. It's for sword fights with pirates." He stood with his feet spread, the walking stick in both hands like a weapon.

William jumped up and down with excitement. "Are there pirates in here?"

Delilah shook her head. "No pirates. But I do have some cookies to put in the oven at the bakery. You want to help?"

William looked at her with suspicion. "Dog cookies or people cookies?"

"Both," she said. "You help me with the dog cookies, and then we can make some people cookies as a reward."

"I can eat them for breakfast?"

"For breakfast."

William gave a little whoop, his hair flying as he jumped into the air.

"Can you get Melody started when she arrives?" she asked.

"I will."

"Watch for pirates!" William said. "I want to help you fight them!"

"Will do, cap'n!"

The boy and Delilah headed out the back door again. The cut between the two stores had been covered with a tarp, so it was impassable, even though you could see the blurry image of the other store through the plastic.

Cody stood in the quiet of the room. He realized he was leaning heavily on his stick and straightened up.

The workout and poor sleep were already pulling at him.

He took in a deep breath. *Stand tall.* He remembered that one, said over and over again by one of the physical therapists. *Don't sink down into your problems.*

He would stand tall. He would show Melody around. And depending on how things went, maybe he would stay to help.

CHAPTER 7

*S*chool was out, and Melody had said her tearful goodbye to her students, hugging the graduating seniors as they stood in line to enter the football stadium. At least she had the previous year's experience to guide her and knew to carry a packet of Kleenex in her purse to make it through the ceremony.

To chase the blues away, she'd messaged Delilah to say she would start painting first thing Saturday morning instead of Monday.

As she got ready that morning, Melody was torn. On one hand, she hated denying Mistletoe the ability to see Tyrus. But on the other hand, she really needed to get her work done, and trying to chaperone the two dogs, both of whom behaved completely out of character around each other, might disrupt her ability to concentrate, especially if she was up on a ladder.

The Pomeranian seemed to know something was up. Maybe it was because Melody had not dressed in the same sort of outfit she would wear to school. Or because the timing was a little off. Melody was always at school by the crack of dawn to organize both her classes and her pep squad. Delilah was meeting her a little later than her usual day, just before the shop opened.

Or maybe it was that Melody was just a bit jittery. Seeing Cody again had her off-kilter. She didn't want to say the wrong thing, and she had blown it the last time they were together.

Despite all this, Melody was anxious to see him again. Sure, it could be difficult. But there was something underneath the surface of him that appealed to her. She felt certain that if she could keep him laughing, the fun, easy-going side of Cody would stay with her. He wouldn't turn into the dark, brooding version.

Not that this didn't have appeal. She had dated more than her fair share of bad boys.

She pulled a red Kong dog toy down from the top of the refrigerator. It was the bonus super deluxe special treat for Mistletoe, especially when it was filled with peanut butter.

Mistletoe began to jump around when she spotted the toy, and let out a little yip when she smelled the peanut butter.

As Melody set it on the floor, she told Mistletoe, "I promise that if today goes well, I'll see about bringing you next time. Deal?"

Mistletoe paid her no mind, of course, already nose-deep into the Kong.

Melody made sure the doggy door to the back yard was unlatched, and quietly tiptoed to the front. Mistletoe remained engrossed with her peanut butter as

Melody slipped outside and strode off down the sidewalk toward Town Square.

The door to the expansion was propped open with the rag again. Melody peeked inside. The front section of the store was quiet, and the shop lamps were gone. They must have been Stanley's. But a tall ladder stood in the center of the room, and a stack of drop cloths, as well as several paint cans topped with different sized brushes, sat in the front corner.

"Hello?" she called.

Tyrus appeared in the doorway.

"Hi, boy," she said. "Where's Cody? Her heart beat so unnaturally loud, she was afraid Cody would be able to hear it.

"I'm back here," Cody said. "Trying to find the tape so we can mark off the line between the red and the white paint."

Melody hurried to the back. Cody was bent over a box, searching through its contents.

"What color is it?"

"Blue," Cody said.

The two of them searched side-by-side.

Melody tried to figure out a way to apologize for not thinking about what she was saying the last time they saw each other. She should've known not to ask him about an embarrassing trait. Usually, she had more common sense than that.

But as they found the tape, and the two of them discussed the order of how they would work around each other to paint the interior of the shop, Melody felt the moment had passed.

They moved straight into the work, Melody running up and down the ladders, and Cody advising her from the floor.

The hours passed quickly, and their progress was easy to assess as the tapeline lengthened along the walls. When the entire room was marked off, the two of them stood in the center examining it to make sure it seemed even and straight.

"It looks like the building may have shifted a little in the back corner, or else that wall was never plumbed perfectly," Cody said, his hand running across the bristles on his cheek.

Melody had to drag her eyes away. She turned to the corner.

"I see what you mean. Even though we know our line is straight there is an optical illusion that it's running uphill."

"Exactly. Do you think we should leave it technically correct, or adjust it so that it is visually appealing?"

Melody planted her hands on her hips and tilted her head. "I think we should go with what *looks* right over what *is* right."

"I agree," Cody said. He glanced at his watch. "I say we fix this, and then we head down to Betty's tea shop. Mom arranged for us to have lunch there. On her."

"That's sweet of her," Melody said. She stepped back up onto the ladder and peeled the end of the blue tape away from the wall. "Since we're just eyeballing it, you'll need to tell me how to move it."

"Bring it down about an inch on the end."

Melody made the adjustment. "How's that?"

"Up just a smidge."

Melody grinned inwardly at the old-fashioned word *smidge*. You could tell Cody had been back in Apple-bottom for a while.

She looked down at him. He gave her an easy grin, and her heart sparked. This was going a lot better than last time.

"Now just fix the other corner so it lines up, and I think we've got it," he said.

The ladder wasn't in quite the right position for her to reach the corner, but she didn't feel like going down to move it and climbing back up again. So Melody leaned hard against the upper level of the ladder, stretching her fingers to the end of the tape.

"Easy there," Cody said. "Sure you don't want to come down and move it?"

"No, I've got it."

Her fingers grazed the end of the tape and pulled it free. Now to just put it back down in line with the other.

She managed to straighten the tape, but the push to flatten it back against the wall took her one inch too far. She felt her balance falter and let out a little squeak of fear.

"Hold on!" Cody called.

Then his hands were grasping her legs, just above the knees. His gentle push rebalanced her weight, and she was able to right herself. She braced herself against the wall and took in a deep breath.

It was more than just the jolt of almost falling. His hands were on her bare legs, his strong fingers ensuring she was balanced again. Her whole body zinged with the contact and continued buzzing even after he let go.

"You okay?" Cody asked.

"I'm good. A little annoyed with myself, that's all."

And she was. Here she all but bragged about her cheerleading gymnastics, and she couldn't even balance herself on the ladder without almost crashing to the ground.

But it might have been worth it to get them a little closer.

Cody looked up at the tape. "Well, it looks like you got it done. The two ends are lined up."

Small mercy. Melody quickly descended the ladder. Cody seemed perfectly happy to skip over the fact that she'd nearly fallen, still peering up at the blue tapeline.

"This looks good. We can pop over and have Mom check it out before we actually start the painting. I bet you can knock out a good amount of it this afternoon."

They walked to the front, and Cody pulled the rag from the door.

As they headed down to Tea for Two, Melody noticed more than one face peering out at them from inside the shops. Gertrude, in particular, gave them a good hard stare as they walked by the pie bakery. She always did want to know all the goings-on in Applebottom. Melody had figured that out within a few months of arriving in town.

She was an interesting lady, every bit of seventy-years-old and as crotchety as all get out. But Melody suspected, as many people in town did, that somewhere deep down, Gertrude was a softy.

Melody gave her a little wave, but the woman quickly looked down at the pie plate she was wiping. Melody had no doubt that in five minutes or less, the fact she was walking through Town Square with Cody Jones would be the talk of Applebottom.

CHAPTER 8

When Cody walked into Tea for Two with Melody, the owner, Betty, sat on the stool behind the counter. She was known around town for her jazzy active wear that matched the bows on her white poodle Clementine. She was one of the kinder, gentler souls of Applebottom, and a town matriarch, having a long line of kids and grandkids that had remained in town.

She slid off her stool, still quite spry for seventy-five. "Why, hello there." She leaned over the counter to look at Tyrus. "And you are such a big doggy. What is his name again?"

"Tyrus," Cody said.

"That's right. Delilah said to feed you two whatever would keep you going. What would you like?"

Neither of them picked up the pink laminated menus from the counter. Cody had been there millions of times, often wandering in for lunch as a kid when he was stuck hanging out at the bakery with his mother.

59

He didn't know about Melody, though. She'd been in Applebottom, what? Two years, she'd said? She might not have a favorite.

But Melody pressed up against the counter. "Betty, you know I can't live without your chicken salad sandwiches."

"I do," she said. "Fruit as usual?"

Melody nodded.

"Lemonade, sweetie?"

"I'm feeling like Applebottom blend as hot tea."

Betty nodded. "What about you, Cody? It's been quite a while since I made a PB&J special for you."

"Aw, Betty, that's what I had as a tyke."

Her eyes twinkled. "You're still a tyke to me."

Cody leaned on his walking stick. "You still have that good pepper jack cheese? The one that goes great with ham?"

"I sure do," she said. "That was extra slices of both, yes? And kettle chips?"

"You've got my number," he said. "I'll do lemonade."

Betty pushed away from the counter and opened the cooler below the chef case. "I have a lovely lemon cake, fresh today," she said. "Can I interest both of you in a slice?"

Cody figured that Melody would be one of those girls perpetually on a diet and would say no, but she surprised him by saying, "Oh yes. And make it a nice thick one."

Betty smiled. "You two settle yourself in. I'll bring it to you."

The shop was empty except for one elderly man

sitting near the window. He had a steaming cup of coffee and a slice of what Cody assumed was the lemon cake Betty was talking about.

It took Cody a moment to place the man. Alfred Felmont. He was a sort of recluse in Applebottom, a widower longer than Cody had been alive, and no family in town. He rarely left his enormous mansion on Table Rock Lake.

Melody also chose a table near the window. As they settled into their chairs, Cody said to Alfred, "Nice seeing you around town."

"It's a pleasant day," Alfred said. He was definitely a distinguished looking man, his steely gray beard and mustache impeccably trimmed. He wore a funny little cap and a suit jacket, even at noon on a Saturday. They didn't make many men like him anymore.

Betty brought them their drinks, Melody's steaming cup and Cody's slender, clear glass.

"Sounds like we plan to paint when we get back," Melody said.

"Yeah. We'll check the lines one more time with a fresh perspective, then I'd say just hit it with the red paint."

They sat in silence for a little while, sipping their drinks. Tyrus settled beneath the table, his tail occasionally thumping on the floor.

Cody hadn't done anything like this since he'd been back. There was decadence to just sitting quietly and eating lunch. For years, meals had been more or less on the run, taken in camps or an overcrowded mess hall in a temporary building.

Ever since he'd been back, he preferred to eat alone, sitting on a makeshift table at the back of the renovation or in his rented house. His mom insisted on Sunday dinners, and he obliged, but overall, his life had been solitary. He hadn't just sat by a public window and watched people go by.

Melody leaned in conspiratorially. "Who is that gentleman sitting at the next table?" she whispered.

That was one part of his small town manners he had completely forgotten. Introductions. "Sorry," he muttered. He turned to Alfred. "Alfred, this is Melody Hopkins. She says you two have never met."

Alfred set down his mug. "I haven't had the pleasure."

Melody waved to him from the other side of the table. "I teach up at the high school."

"How lovely," Alfred said. "Always nice to see fresh faces about town."

Betty brought their sandwiches, and Melody took a giant bite, groaning a little. "I was so hungry. I've been living off of ramen and lettuce."

As soon as she said it, her jaw froze, as if she hadn't intended to say something so revealing.

"That sounds like a college diet," Cody said. "Do they pay you up there at the high school?"

Melody's eyes widened into big circles above the sandwich she clutched in both hands. "Oh, they do. Just college loans and all that."

But something about the way she said it pricked his concern. "Is that why you're taking on extra work during summer break?"

She took another big bite of sandwich, and he was pretty sure it was so she had time to think about the answer to his question. Interesting. She'd told him before she really, *really* needed the money.

He held her gaze, not letting her off the hook, even as she chewed and swallowed the bite.

"I have some extra expenses," she said. She picked up her tea and took a sip, gathering her thoughts again.

Cody set down his sandwich and folded his hands together, elbows braced on the table. He had all day. It was interesting to see Melody have any sort of vulnerability. She seemed like a superstar. Cheerleader. Teacher. The pep squad coach.

Melody's eyes dropped to her cup. "It's my grandmother," she said. "She's in," she hesitated, "a sort of assisted living situation. Medicare wasn't paying for much by way of comfort, so I upgraded her situation."

Cody's eyebrows lifted. "That's got to be expensive."

She held her mug close to her face. "It's worth it."

He sensed there was more to the story, but he didn't press. "Well, I think it's admirable you stepped up to help. Where is your family?"

"My parents are divorced and have been since I was little. Dad lives in Arkansas. He writes software. Mom is down in Oklahoma. She teaches preschool."

"And this grandmother belongs to…"

"My mom's mom. Grandma lives about an hour from here."

"There weren't any places near your mom? I'm betting you drive up there a lot."

Melody gulped her tea. "I do. Every weekend. I'll be

going there tomorrow afternoon. She loves Mistletoe. The staff is great. They let me bring her."

"That's nice."

Cody watched the interplay of emotions that crossed Melody's face. The girl was an open book. She picked up her sandwich and looked at it, her appetite seeming to have fled. This told Cody that there was something up with the grandmother. Maybe she was sick. Maybe assisted living was a code word for hospice or something like that.

Then, an expression of hardened determination took over. She bit sharply into the sandwich. Cody got that, too. It wasn't ramen or lettuce, so she felt compelled to finish it, even if she didn't want to.

There was more to this girl than he thought.

At the next table over, Alfred carefully picked up his empty plate and cup. He turned to them with a little bow. "So nice to see you both today. Have a lovely afternoon."

Cody nodded at him. "See you around town, Mr. Felmont."

"Such a pleasure to meet you," Melody said.

Alfred carefully placed his dishes into the basin. He was about to go out the door when he suddenly took a step back. The motion caught Cody's attention and he looked out the window. Gertrude was barreling across Town Square, holding a small container.

"She's looking spry today," Melody said.

It was true. Gertrude was booking it across the street, paying no mind to traffic. She hustled down the sidewalk and burst through the door of Tea for Two, breathing heavy.

Alfred had stepped to the side of the door to get out of her way. Gertrude blew right past him, spotting Betty. "Did he leave already?"

Betty tried to subtly point a finger back at the door.

Gertrude whirled around and sucked in a breath at seeing Alfred.

"Good afternoon, Ms. Vogel," he said.

Gertrude seemed frozen in place. She held onto the clear plastic container like it was the last MRE in a combat zone.

She stood there staring for a moment, then seemed to remember what she was holding. She thrust the box at Alfred. "For you."

Alfred accepted it. He did not seem surprised by any part of this exchange, as if it was a common occurrence. "Why, thank you," he said, bowing his head slightly.

The two of them stood there a moment, then Gertrude seemed to snap out of it. "Well, I best get back to the pie shop before someone steals the meringue right from under me."

She glanced around at all of them, finally seeming to take note of Cody and Melody, and rushed back out the door.

Betty could barely contain herself from busting out laughing. Cody assumed this was some long-standing situation.

He realized Melody had finished her sandwich. He gulped down the rest of his lemonade as Alfred left the tea shop. When the door had completely closed, Melody said, "Well, that was adorable."

"Did you see what she brought him?" he asked.

Betty spoke from behind the counter. "Lemon meringue pie." Her eyes focused out the windows at Alfred's retreating figure "She makes one for him every single day, just in the hope he might stop by."

"How did she know he was here?" Cody asked.

"I told her," Betty said. "You don't live in Applebottom long without knowing that if you spot Alfred Felmont on his rare appearance in town, you better let Gertrude know. Because if you don't..." Betty shook her head.

"She might poison your apple pie?" Cody ventured.

"Not quite." She gave him a sly smile. "But close. Very close."

"You ready?" Melody asked.

"Yeah."

They stood. Cody had to organize himself, getting Tyrus's leash and his walking stick in one hand, picking up his plate with the other.

Betty rushed to the table. "I've got all this. You guys get back to Delilah's. I can't wait to see what you do."

Cody set his plate down and backed away. The people of Applebottom were certainly accommodating. He wondered if his mother had warned the town about his limitations. And his moods.

But he civilly said, "Thank you," and led Tyrus to the door.

Melody stacked all their plates. "Yes, thank you. It was delicious."

They headed up the Square. Small towns were definitely a different sort of beast, that was for sure. But as he walked through the summer sunshine with Melody at his side and Tyrus trotting along, he thought to himself, *Maybe this isn't so bad.*

CHAPTER 9

*T*he first afternoon Melody painted at the top of the ladder went incredibly fast. She'd intended to leave at her usual end-of-school time to keep Mistletoe on schedule, but only when Cody approached her to say it was after four did she realize how many hours had passed.

After two years of being on display when she worked, teaching math classes and coaching pep squad, it was nice to do something where no one paid any attention to her as she did her job.

Or *mostly* didn't.

Sometimes she could feel Cody's eyes on her as she covered the dingy gray walls with the bright red paint. They'd turned some corner in their friendship. She could feel it. She had told him about her grandmother, something she'd kept to herself.

Melody wasn't really sure why she'd made it a secret. Maybe because dying grandmothers didn't make for cheerful conversation, and one thing she always tried to do was be a bright spot in people's day. It was compulsive. She couldn't help it.

But the truth of the matter was her grandmother being so close to the end was one of the few really difficult things to ever happen to her. Her parents had separated when she was very small, and she didn't really remember the break. They were kind to each other, even though they were apart, and Melody never really felt a negative pull when visiting one or the other.

Her father had regularly driven down to her cheer competitions or to watch her perform at football games. Both parents had been there for her, cordially sitting next to each other.

No, Grandma was definitely the first great tragedy she was going to experience.

Just thinking of Grandma with her halo of puffy gray hair, her pink housecoat and wrinkled smiling eyes, brought Melody down a notch. She finished the corner, and Cody held the ladder steady as she made her way down.

"Full day," he said. "I assume you'll skip tomorrow since you're going to see your grandmother?"

"Definitely," she said. "What time should I be here Monday?"

"Whenever you like. Just let me know so Mom or I can open up for you."

"Nine o'clock is good," she said. "I might try bringing Mistletoe. If it doesn't work, I can always walk her home."

Cody shrugged his shoulders. "I'm sure it will be fine. Tyrus will cozy up to her the whole day."

At his name, the golden retriever lumbered over and pressed his head beneath Cody's hand.

"Such a sweetie," Melody said.

"He was trained by the best."

"That must be a great job, training therapy dogs."

"Most of them are volunteers."

"How wonderful."

Cody held out his hand to take the brush from Melody. "I'll wash this. You can head on out. I'm sure your dog is anxious to see you."

He was probably right about that. Melody passed him the brush and the open paint can, wondering how he would carry them and also walk with his stick.

But he was proficient at that, using his hand to hang onto the brush and walking stick, and dangling the can in his free hand.

"See you Monday," she said. "I look forward to it." And she meant it.

Cody gave her a quick nod, but she could see a happy gleam in his eye. He and Tyrus disappeared into the back, and Melody hurried home to Mistletoe.

She finally understood the phrase *I have a song in my heart.*

Melody thought of Cody as she drove out to the nursing home the next day. He definitely seemed changed after their lunch. This was going better than she expected.

All the way, with Mistletoe asleep in her carrier, Melody looked with wonder upon the gorgeous landscape, majestic trees, lakes, and the foothills of the Ozark Mountains. She imagined what she would say to Cody about each one. In fact, she didn't realize she was actually speaking a running commentary out loud until Mistletoe peered over the top of the zippered enclosure of the carrier as if to say, *"What, Mama?"*

Melody laughed at herself and petted the little dog's head until she settled down again.

When they arrived at the nursing home, Melody kept Mistletoe in the carrier while she checked in at the desk. She would have to stay in the gardens with the dog, but the staff would bring her grandmother outside. The weather was beautiful, perfect for some air and sunshine.

She left the empty carrier on a bench, and the two of them strolled the manicured circle behind the building while they waited. Mistletoe dashed from one bush to another, sniffing.

At last, Melody spotted one of the staff members walking alongside her grandmother, who still insisted she did not need a walker or a wheelchair even though her steps were halting and slow.

She was dressed in lilac pants and one of her favorite floral blouses. She carried a white sweater over her arm even though there was not even a hint of chill in the air. As it always did, Melody's heart caught to see her.

Her arms were thin, and her shoulders a little stooped. But when she spotted Melody, her eyes crinkled and she smiled, and that was the most important thing.

Melody watched the care the staff member took to

help her grandmother to her seat. Grandma looked serene and happy as the two of them sat on a cushioned bench a little ways from the door. Every penny Melody was spending to keep her grandmother here was worth it. The gardens. The homelike atmosphere. This was what she wanted for her grandmother as she lived out her last days.

The cancer was a slow-moving one, but it progressed all the same. Melody would stop by for a report when she left. There had been tests last week, this she knew, as she had designated herself the primary family caregiver. The last life expectancy she had seen was three to six months, which she knew was just a number. Grandma could last much longer, or take a sudden turn.

With luck and prayers, she would still be here at Christmas. The holidays were Grandma's absolute favorite season, and Melody had named her dog Mistletoe because of it. She could only hope Grandma would be there to see one more.

"Come on Mistletoe," she said, tugging on the leash.

They completed the circle that brought them back around to the rear of the building.

"You two catch up," the woman said. "I'll check in about an hour from now."

Normally the staff left them together for as long as they wanted. Limiting it to an hour was new. A tendril of concern shifted through Melody.

She plunked down in the spot the woman had vacated and took her grandmother's hand. "How are you, Grandma?"

"Fit as a fiddle," Grandma said, her common response.

"Good."

Mistletoe hopped up onto the bench, snuggling in between them.

Grandma released Melody's hand to pet the fluffy dog. "And how is our Mistletoe?"

"Ornery as ever," Melody said.

Her conversations with her grandmother always started out the same, with the genteel pleasantries she'd grown up with. When they reached the end of those, Melody would ask for a particular story for Grandma to relate, or sometimes her grandmother had saved up one she'd remembered Melody had never heard before.

"So what are you going to tell me about today?" Melody asked.

But instead of launching into a talk, her grandmother searched Melody's face with a wise, penetrating intensity. "Something's happened to you," she said. "Was graduation difficult this year?" She reached out to touch Melody's cheek.

"A little. I think I did better than last year, though."

"A favored child leave you?"

"Oh, several. It was a good year."

"Hmmm."

Before her grandmother could guess that she'd met someone, Melody quickly asked, "What have *you* been doing this last week?"

"Making Christmas ornaments."

"In June?"

"They have a Christmas in July here. So we start decorations early."

"Why?"

Grandma's eyes met hers with sadness. "Because many of us won't see another holiday season."

Melody's throat went dry. "But you will."

"Maybe." Grandma patted her hand. "But don't you fret about that."

Melody couldn't speak. The thought of the world without her grandmother was too much to bear.

Her grandmother's gaze never wavered. "So what else is new with you? Something big, I think."

Melody knew exactly what she was seeing. If keeping a cheerful attitude was her superpower, hiding her emotions was definitely her kryptonite.

She gave in. "I took on a summer job helping out a woman who owns a dog bakery. Some easy stuff, painting the walls, stenciling paw prints. It's been fun."

"Aw, that would explain this." She lifted Melody's hand where a few flecks of paint still clung to her nails.

"Exactly. I want to try taking Mistletoe tomorrow, but there is another dog there so I might be too distracted."

"Distracted by dogs, huh?" Grandma wasn't fooled.

Melody relented. She might as well tell her everything. "There's someone else working in the store. A young man named Cody. He's the son of the woman who owns the bakery."

"How old?"

"I'd say twenty-four or so."

Her grandmother sat back against the bench. "Now we're getting somewhere."

Melody stared down at her lap. How could she describe Cody? That he was dark and brooding, but also funny and sweet? It wouldn't make any sense.

"Tell me about him," Grandma prompted.

She'd have to give it a shot. "We like the same music," she said.

"That must make the hours go by faster."

"It does," Melody said. "We both work to 80s rock."

"I remember that music," Grandma said. "Your mother kept it blasting day and night."

Melody saw her opportunity to change the subject. "I bet she did. Did it drive you crazy?"

"All the time. I remember one band called Mouse, I think?"

"Ratt?"

"Oh yes, that was it. They sang *Round and Round.*"

And the conversation was off and running, Grandma relating funny stories about Melody's mother's high school days. Melody sat in contentment, listening to her grandmother's voice, the June sunshine beaming down and the bright flowers blooming in every direction.

And she'd told her about Cody. Just a little. Just enough.

Mistletoe settled down between them and fell asleep in the sun.

For Melody, this was pretty much the definition of heaven.

CHAPTER 10

On Monday morning, Cody dug around in his closet until he located his Metallica T-shirt. He knew Melody would notice. He had quite a collection of heavy metal band T-shirts, most of them re-issued as the music returned in popularity after so many decades. Everything really did come back around again.

When he and Tyrus unlocked the rear door of the expansion, his mother poked her head out the back of her bakery.

"How did you know I was coming in?" he asked.

Cody expected her to say, "Mother's intuition," but she surprised him. "Your father installed one of those little beeping alarms. It goes off in my shop when the back door opens to this one. I wanted it for the days when I'm all alone and tending both spaces."

"Do you have Billy?"

"No, your sister has him in camp this week."

Delilah entered the new shop, and the two of them

made their way through the chaos of the back room, flipping on lights as they went. When they reached the actual store area, Delilah clapped her hands at the bright-white walls topped in red. "You two have made a lot of progress."

"You want me to start building the counter?"

"That's a good idea." She brushed her fingers along one wall. "I've been trying to decide what we should do for the grand opening."

Cody sat down on the top of the stepstool. His leg was bothering him extra today. "You mean like a special event?"

"Maybe," she said. "Do you think we need it? I mean, everybody in Applebottom is going to know it's opening."

"I seem to recall that this town likes any excuse for a celebration," Cody said.

"Ain't that the truth," Delilah said. "Gertrude will want to make her pies, and Betty her teacakes. Danny and Topher will do up some flower arrangements."

"Seems like we ought to give them their chance." Cody watched the front door. It was time for Melody to arrive, and he wondered if his mother was trying to snoop on them.

"People could bring their dogs, too. Like a pet party."

"That all sounds fine," Cody said. "Are you gonna have a theme?"

"I don't know." Delilah wandered the space with her arms crossed. "I'll think of something. Do you think we should scrape the paint off these windows yet?"

"I say leave it until you're ready for people to look in. Maybe after the counters are up and the place looks more finished." He left out the part that he liked the privacy with Melody. Everybody would walk by and peer in all the time otherwise.

His mother gazed back at him fondly. "It sure is nice having you here. Are you getting along with Melody?"

Now she was warming up to what she wanted to know. Cody petted Tyrus on the head to avoid looking his mother in the eye. "She's all right. She works hard." Betty had probably given her a full report about their lunch on Saturday.

Gossip about single people was irresistible. Look what they did with poor Alfred, summoning Gertrude for a pie ambush.

"How long do you think it's going to take?" his mom asked.

"The walls were fast, but the detail work will take more time," he said. "We need to finish out the door and paint the trim. The counter will need to be constructed and painted. Once the shelves are in, you'll want to take a look and decide if you want to keep them silver or paint them, too."

Delilah nodded. She walked closer and patted him on the shoulder. "I trust you two will do a great job," she said. "I better get back to the bakery before something burns."

She'd no more left when Cody heard a small tap on the front glass. He'd forgotten to put the rag out to prop the door open.

He stumbled in his hurry to get to the door, glad for the painted windows that hid his clumsiness. Melody stood outside in jean shorts and a pink T-shirt that had seen better days. Good working clothes.

He stepped aside to let her in. "Ready to hit it again?"

"Yeah," she said. "Do you think I should do the paw prints, or are we going to try to tackle the new door between the stores?"

Her dark hair swung in a loose ponytail. Old white sneakers were already covered with several different colors of paint. He hadn't noticed them Saturday. After a day apart, he wanted to memorize everything about her.

"I'll start building the counter," he said. "The boards are already cut and ready. I was just waiting for the wall behind it to be painted. Why don't you hit the baseboards first, then take a look at the little public bathroom? All the fixtures are going to remain the same, but it certainly needs freshening up in there with paint."

"Okay," she said. "Baseboards white, I assume?"

"I think so. The red might be tricky."

Melody tilted her head, looking over the walls. "I'm pretty good at tricky. But I agree that red on top and bottom might be too much."

"There should be a nice high-gloss white back there. We're going to use it for the counter too. Should be pretty tough and withstand things bumping it without chipping."

"I should still probably apply a couple of coats, don't you think?"

"I would." He moved slowly toward a box by the

wall. Dang it, he was so much more crippled up than usual today. He withdrew a couple of rolls of painter's tape. "The baseboards are laid out on tarps, but you'll want to mark off the sink and things in the bathroom." He tossed the rolls to her.

She caught them both neatly. "Will do."

They worked separately throughout the morning, although Cody was always acutely aware of her proximity. Close to noon, Delilah popped over with two box lunches from Annabelle's Café.

"Thought I'd mix it up a little today," she said. "Melody, Flo knew what you always ordered, and I could pick things out for Cody in my sleep, of course." She handed them each a box. "Feel free to go somewhere else to eat them. I'm not asking you to work through lunch or anything."

"Thanks," Melody said, peeking in her box. "Braised beef. The best."

"Good." His mother twisted her hands in front of her *Stay at Home Dog Mom* T-shirt. She seemed nervous. "It sure is looking good in here. I'll just skedaddle." She hurried out the back.

When she was gone, Melody turned to Cody with a laugh. "Skedaddle?"

"Well, you know in Applebottom it's always 1954."

"Are you at a stopping point?" Melody asked.

"Close enough," he said. "Did you want to go somewhere or eat these here?"

Melody twisted her ponytail around a finger. "I get the feeling the town is spying on us. Do you?"

"Definitely," Cody said. "And the fact that she

ordered this from Annabelle's means they're all talking about us over there. Sometimes I wish I could be anonymous."

"It's not all it's cracked up to be," Melody said. "I went to a gigantic university, and I would've been lost without the cheerleaders. I don't know how I would've made friends. The classes were all so huge, and none of your professors ever knew you."

"I guess there are drawbacks to both," he said. "You want to stay here behind our painted windows?"

"Actually, I might check up on Mistletoe, if that's okay. She noticed that I wasn't dressed for school and worked herself up into a tizzy when I left."

"I thought you were bringing her today."

"She was in a mood. But maybe I'll bring her back with me this afternoon if she's calmed down."

Cody hid his disappointment. He'd been looking forward to another lunch with her. "That's fine. Tyrus and I can just hang out here."

"We could walk together. I'm sure Tyrus would be happy to see Mistletoe. There's a picnic bench in my backyard. With a privacy fence." She gave him a half smile, and even though it would be a long, slow walk, Cody could not have said no to her if she'd asked him to climb Mount Everest.

"Okay. Let me leash up Tyrus."

"I'll carry the boxes," she said, "since you'll have Tyrus on the leash."

She'd done that on purpose, Cody realized as he passed her the box. She knew he'd have trouble managing his stick, the leash, and a box for a long walk. And the way he was feeling today, it would be even more of a trial than usual.

But he wanted to give it a shot. He could at least make a stab at a normal moment with an incredibly beautiful girl who'd invited him to her house.

They set off out the back door, avoiding Town Square and prying eyes. They walked down back streets, turning their faces to the sun after a morning indoors.

Melody took it slow, pausing to admire flowers and bushes and the odd bit of stonework. Perhaps she would've done that anyway, but Cody felt she was trying to make the walk easier on him by clearly not being in a rush.

Tyrus kept close as Cody moved along the walk. Sweat broke out on his forehead as he began to tire out. It was ridiculous, really. He could work out harder than anyone in a closed room, but ask him to travel more than a few blocks, and everything seemed to give up the ghost.

But this was exactly what he should be doing. Walking distances. Pushing himself rather than merely lifting weights. He just hadn't felt particularly motivated to get out and show off his lack of mobility.

"This is it," Melody said, turning up the sidewalk to a cute white house with pale green trim. It suited her.

A red and blue sign by the steps proclaimed her Applebottom Pride. Cody used to have a similar sign in his yard. She definitely kept her school spirit on display.

Mistletoe leaped up Melody's legs as soon as the door opened, but when she saw Tyrus, she abandoned her owner for the retriever. The two of them turned in circles together, sniffing and making little happy barks as if they hadn't seen each other in years.

"There's definitely something going on with those two," Melody said.

"We'll have to chaperone them or people will talk."

Melody laughed; a happy sound that filled her house as they passed through. The front room was simple and tidy with a floral sofa and matching pale-green chair. A big white bookcase was topped with a megaphone and two sets of pom-poms in different colors. High school and college, he surmised.

They walked into a bright kitchen painted yellow and green. This room was not nearly as neat as the other.

"Please excuse all the dishes," Melody said. "The end of school wrecked me and I haven't caught up yet."

So she did have a flaw. He grinned to himself at the pile of pots and plates in the sink spilling out onto the counters. He imagined himself saying, "You cook, I'll clean," and couldn't hold back the chuckle.

"What?" Melody asked in mock indignation. "Is my messiness amusing?"

"It's adorable," he said.

"My mother wouldn't think so. She'd say I was raised in a barn."

They continued out the back door and into a spacious yard. The grass was thick and green, and a simple wooden picnic table sat under the expansive branches of an Elm tree.

Melody set the boxes on the table. "My little slice of heaven," she said. "Whoever had this house before me had the greenest thumb, and this grass has been unstoppable even during the Applebottom summers."

"Who mows it?"

"I do," she said. "I don't play the damsel in distress."

"Other than when you're falling off ladders?"

Her cheeks colored pink.

"I'm sorry," he said quickly. "I didn't mean to embarrass you."

"No, it's fine. It was a funny moment."

Their eyes held a minute. Cody remembered the feel of her when he caught her and wondered if she was thinking of it, too.

A bird flitted to a low branch and Mistletoe went nuts barking at it. Tyrus sat on his haunches, watching the Pomeranian with amusement. He was well trained.

"It's a great space," he said. "Mom's yard is always half dirt because the dogs dig everything up."

"Do you live with her?"

"No, I rent a place about six blocks from here."

Melody sat on the bench. "Mistletoe will occasionally go after something in that rose garden in the back corner," she said, waving her hand in that direction. "But overall, she's pretty good."

Cody swung his leg over the seat of the picnic table and rested his walking stick against the side. They unpacked their boxes and talked of inconsequential things, the weather, and places around town.

The sun filtered through the leaves and fell on Melody's hair. The dogs lounged in the sun, and Cody was pretty sure, lately, every day was better than the last.

CHAPTER 11

*T*he week settled into an easy pattern. Cody would arrive first and unlock the expansion, leaving the rag in the door for Melody to open.

He would busy himself with some small task until she arrived, and the two of them would review the previous day's work, and either pick up where they'd left off or make a new plan.

His mom frequently came over with either lunch or a suggestion about where to go in town where she had prearranged their meal to be covered.

Over those days, Cody found himself relaxing in Melody's presence. He liked her, and certainly, she was friendly and easy-going with him. He wondered if he should try to stir up the courage to ask her to go somewhere other than an arranged lunch, but things were working so well, he didn't want to make things awkward between them if she turned him down.

On Thursday afternoon of that first week, his

mother wrestled with the plastic tarp between the two stores, finally tearing it down. "I'm done going out the back door and in the other," she said as the two of them popped their heads up from the detail work they were applying to the checkout counter.

"It's getting finished enough in here that it's not terrible when someone pops a head in," Cody said. "As long as we don't stock the shelves, they'll realize that it's not open yet."

"Good," his mother said, crumpling the plastic beneath her arms. "I've been talking to some of the other pet store owners in the area, and I found out there's a pet parade this Saturday in Galena. It's about an hour drive, but I thought it might be fun to check it out. Maybe we could do something similar."

Melody set her brush in the paint tray. "Are you thinking of a Fourth of July parade?"

"I'm not sure we can be ready by the Fourth of July. That's just three weeks away. She glanced around. "No, I can't get the stock in that quick. I need at least six weeks."

"I think a pet parade could happen anytime," Cody said. "You want me to come along?"

"Both of you, if I can have you. Bring your dogs. Make a day of it. The two of you would be instrumental in helping me organize it."

"Has there ever been a pet parade in Applebottom?" Melody asked.

"Not that I can recall," Delilah said. "And I've been here going on thirty years. Gertrude would know for sure. But it's been plenty long enough for it to be a novelty. If we could get Savannah on board, we could showcase a bunch of her adoptable dogs. She could wrangle some volunteers."

"It sounds cute," Melody said. "I'd be happy to help. I'm here all summer."

Cody sighed. If nobody could see why walking a pet parade might be a trial for him, he wouldn't bring it up. "What time are we leaving on Saturday?"

"Let's all meet behind the shop at nine," she said. "I'll bring lunch for all of us." Someone entered her side of the shop, so she quickly disappeared back through the door.

"I think it sounds fun," Melody said.

Cody shrugged. Sure, for most people, a walk with their pets did sound like a fun morning. But most of them had two good legs.

&.

On Saturday morning, Melody walked up to the back of the shop with Mistletoe. Delilah's big white van was already parked near the door. Cody's green Jeep wasn't there yet.

"Come along, Mistletoe," she told the dog, who had picked up Tyrus's scent, no doubt, and was straining for the back door of the expansion instead. "Tyrus isn't here. You'll see him in a minute."

Her dog had it bad. She'd never seen Mistletoe act like this. Sure, there were dogs she was friendly with. A few of them were pups they met repeatedly at Applebottom Park.

And there were ones that she immediately repelled from, usually those that were much bigger, with deep menacing barks.

But this thing with Tyrus was like an obsession.

"They're going to make a movie about you two," she said with a giggle. *"Fatal Doggy Attraction."* She leaned into the open door at the back of the bakery. "Delilah? You there?"

No one answered, but Bruno, Delilah's bulldog, trotted across the room. Bruno and Mistletoe sniffed at each other for a moment, seemed unimpressed, and parted ways.

"I know, you only have eyes for Tyrus," Melody said. She stepped inside, the smell of baking cookies warm and inviting.

A little dinger chimed, and Delilah hurried in from the main shop, stopping short when she saw Melody. "Oh my goodness, is it that time already? Let me just get these on the rack."

Delilah opened the door to a large commercial oven, and Mistletoe leaped forward on her leash as the smell of bacon and warm cookies intensified.

"Whoa there, girl," Melody said. "You're going to burn your sniffer."

Bruno, who was clearly more experienced with the ways of the bakery, sat on his haunches, nose in the air.

Delilah pulled several trays of bone-shaped cookies from the oven and slid them onto narrow metal shelves next to the oven.

"Just waiting on Fred to take over, and Cody to get

here," Delilah said. "The parade is at eleven, so we have plenty of time."

"I've really been looking forward to this," Melody said. "I've never been to a pet parade."

"Well, don't expect anything fancy. I don't think Galena is much bigger than Applebottom. But it will be helpful to see how they organize things."

She bumped the oven closed with her hip. "We'll make ours bigger and better."

Bruno gave out a little *woof*, and the two women turned to see Delilah's husband Fred at the back door.

"Fresh batch on the cooling rack," Delilah told Fred. "Cases are stocked. I prepackaged the orders that typically come in on a Saturday. Just double check that's what they actually want. Sometimes they pick up something new." Her words were breathless, and Fred squeezed her shoulders.

"It's going to be all right, Delilah," Fred said in a soothing voice. He was the chief of the volunteer fire department, and he used that same tone while answering students' panicked questions when he came to speak every year at the high school about prom and graduation nights. Melody had met him many times and knew he was a genuinely great guy.

He nodded at her. "Good morning, Melody. Glad you're going along to keep this wild woman in check."

Melody let out a light laugh. "It's not an easy job, but I assure you, I am up to the task."

Delilah elbowed Fred in the belly. "Oh stop it, you two. If there's a fire call, Fred, just ask Maude to pop over. She knows you're in charge for the day."

Fred squeezed her shoulders again. "Micah is aware of the situation. He can handle a typical call. Only if it's a full-blown fire situation would I need to go out."

He couldn't resist getting one more gentle jab in. "And with you out of town, I'd say the likelihood of big trouble is down seventy-five percent."

"You're a brute," Delilah said, snapping a dish towel at him.

Melody smiled at the couple. That was a relationship goal right there. How long had they been married? Probably close to thirty years. Melody liked how they could good-naturedly kid each other, and it was just part of their love language.

The door banged, and Delilah whipped around. "Oh, there he is. Excellent."

Cody entered through the door with Tyrus. Mistletoe immediately dashed to the end of her leash. Melody had known to keep it coiled tight. Still, the two dogs strained toward each other until Cody moved forward enough that they could touch noses.

Delilah shook her head. "That's true love."

Fred wrapped his arms around her middle. "We know it when we see it."

"Keep the PDA at home, kids," Cody said, but his mouth had an easy smile.

Fred squeezed Delilah even harder. "Boy, we were doing PDA before you were even an idea in our heads. Although, maybe not too long before." He kissed her hair.

Delilah burst out with a raucous laugh. "All right, boys, don't scare Melody away." She pulled away from

Fred. "I have a lunch cooler packed, water and snacks for the dogs, and a little wagon in case they get tired." She glanced up at Cody at that. "I'm not sure how much walking we'll be doing."

Cody pressed both palms into his stick, one hand stacked on the other. "Whatever it is, I can handle it," he said.

Delilah bit her lip. "I'm sure you can."

"Are you guys taking the van?" Fred asked.

Delilah's smile brightened at this. "Of course we are. I don't get to show off my doggy van very often."

Delilah instructed Fred to go pick up the stack of items near the door, and she called Bruno to follow. The whole group of them walked outside to the shiny white doggy bakery van. It had paw prints running across the side.

"Are you going to have 'Pet Store' added to it?" Melody asked.

"Maybe," Delilah said. "Sometimes it doesn't look right when you add stuff after the image is sealed. But I'll look into it."

Fred shoved the cooler and the wagon to one side of the van, and Mistletoe and Tyrus immediately jumped into the back.

"What do you want to do about the dogs?" Cody asked.

"There are safety harnesses back there," Delilah said. "Or we can use the crate. What you think?"

Melody leaned in to pat Mistletoe's head. "As long as these two can get near each other, it will be fine."

"Let's see how Bruno is with the others," Delilah

said. "If it looks like there might be a problem, we can always keep him in the back harness and let your dogs in the back seat with you two."

Melody and Cody glanced at each other at the same time. So his mom was going to chauffeur the two of them like teenagers? That would be something.

Bruno paid the other two dogs no mind as he trotted up the little ramp Fred had set out for him. He sat right next to his oversized harness and waited patiently to be snapped in.

Melody crawled in and clipped in Mistletoe and Tyrus. "You've got quite a lot of harnesses back here," Melody said.

"Sometimes I transport fosters," Delilah said. "Can you fix up Bruno?"

Melody strapped in the burly bulldog. "All good."

Cody leaned in the back to check on the dogs. "Mom, it seems like the dogs are happy here. But I'm going to drive behind you in case Melody needs to get back, or one of the dogs doesn't work out."

Delilah paused, looking at the two of them. "I assume Melody is going to ride with you?"

"Unless you need me to manage the dogs," Melody said. She and Cody had not discussed this, but she could see what he was doing. Delilah would talk their ears off the whole way, and apparently, Cody wanted some time with her. Her heart turned over.

"I've managed as many as ten untrained strays at one time," Delilah said. "I am sure I can handle these three sweet dogs."

Cody gave her a little nod. "It's settled, then. Just pull over if you run into trouble, and I will stop and help."

They headed over to Cody's green Jeep. When he'd started the car and they followed Delilah out from behind the Town Square shops, he said, "I hope this is okay with you."

"No, it's great," she said. "As long as the dogs are good."

"Does Mistletoe travel well?"

"Oh, yes. She'll settle right down."

"So will Tyrus. His big concern will be being away from me. But it will be fine."

Melody's belly flipped again. She hadn't even thought of that. Cody was without his service dog. Was he okay without him?

He must be, or he wouldn't have done it. Nothing about Cody seemed the least bit off. He hadn't even been dark or stony with her since those first couple of meetings. In fact, she was pretty sure that he liked her company. Maybe when they were together, she was the service dog. The thought of herself in a red service made her giggle.

"What's so funny?" Cody asked.

Shoot. How would she get out of this? She did not want to make a conversation mistake as big as the one the other day.

"I was just picturing your mom talking to the dogs the way she would've talked to us if we were in the car with her."

She said a little thank you to her own brain for coming up with that one.

Cody chuckled. "That's exactly what was on my mind when she suggested we ride with her."

Melody looked down at the radio. "So. I'm waiting for you to play some AC/DC," she said.

He gave her a huge grin, and her heart melted another degree. "Your wish is my command."

CHAPTER 12

*A*s Cody drove his Jeep along the highway, Melody at his side, he realized that this was the most normal moment he'd had since his return from the VA Hospital.

Behind the wheel, his walking stick tossed in the back, he felt perfectly ordinary. He and Melody listened to AC/DC, singing along with the lyrics when they knew them, and every time she turned her face to his with a smile, it felt like a miracle.

He could remember moments like these from before, back in high school and that one terrific summer after he graduated before he took off for basic.

And he'd loved being in the service. He'd thrived during training and had felt cool and competent even while deployed. He wasn't a thrill seeker, necessarily, but he believed in a job well done. And in the Army, he'd done exactly that.

Sometimes he blamed rotten luck on what had happened to him. Other times he accepted a certain level of risk, something he'd agreed to take on with his assignment.

He knew nobody was guaranteed anything, even if they were smart and capable and dedicated. And his life had been forever altered in that explosion.

But today he could set all those dark thoughts aside. It was just him, his car, a bright sunshiny day, and this girl.

The signal blinked on his mother's white van ahead of him, and he followed her as she turned off the highway and into a small town. He glanced at the clock. An hour had already passed? It seemed impossible.

"Are we here?" Melody asked.

"Looks like it."

Galena was a typical small town for Missouri, narrow roads with sparse houses. At first, there was no sign anything might be going on today, but as they moved into town, cardboard signs with balloons attached began to appear. "Pet Parade," they announced. "Bring your dogs!"

Melody clapped her hands. "This is exciting," she said. "Do you think there will be many people?"

"It's a nice day. They should have a decent turnout if they did a good job promoting it."

Melody pulled out her phone. "I think those little signs are a great idea." She snapped a couple of shots of them. "They make sure the locals know."

As they drew nearer to the heart of town, evidence of the parade became more obvious. They passed a truck pulling a trailer covered in hay bales and streamers.

"That's easy to do," Melody said. "Surely we know somebody with a trailer."

"Archie, the football announcer, has at least one," Cody said. "He fixes up classic cars and uses a trailer to haul them to shows. In fact, he might drive one of his restoration jobs in the parade. Someone else could drive his truck and trailer."

"I wonder how many members of the pep squad have dogs," Melody said. "We could decorate the float, and then the students could ride on it with their animals."

"You're thinking big already," Cody said. "Mom will love that."

The van pulled over on what appeared to be the town's Main Street.

"She took the last spot," Melody said.

"We'll find something," Cody said. "It's better for her to be close since she has all the supplies and the dogs."

He imagined Melody thinking, *but you have the gimpy leg*, and forced himself not to assume that. Still, his pulse picked up, and when he reached out to pet Tyrus on his head, his dog wasn't there.

Cody drew in a deep breath instead, imagining the circles on the screen of his PTSD device. He turned the corner and spotted an open spot on the side of the road where a couple of other cars had already begun to park.

He slid in behind an old pickup and killed the engine. "Let's go help her release the hounds," he said, hoping his voice sounded light and not as strained as he felt.

If Melody noticed anything, she didn't let on and

practically bounced with excitement as she came around the car to head back to the main drag.

The crumbled edge of the street made for slower going than he would've liked, but when they made it back to the white van, his mom had just opened the back door. "I know you doggies want out. Hold your horses."

Melody rushed forward. "I can crawl in the back and get them." She disappeared into the van.

After a moment, she reappeared with all three leashes. "Can somebody grab these? I'll push the cooler and the wagon closer to the door. They slid a little."

"Here you go, Cody," his mom said. "Try to keep the dogs under control while we unload."

Cody didn't particularly enjoy watching the two women do the work he would have preferred to tackle if he wasn't using a cane, but he did have his hands full. All three dogs attempted to lunge away from him, excited by the prospect of a new place to sniff.

Mistletoe and Tyrus weaved in and around each other, swiftly tangling their lines. Cody was not as free as he could be to shift the leashes around because Bruno was pulling in the opposite direction.

Melody shut the door of the van. "Looks like they're giving you a run for your money," she called out.

"They'll settle in." He managed to hang onto his walking stick as the dogs tried to go their separate ways.

But when Melody approached with the empty wagon, Mistletoe immediately bee-lined for it. Tyrus trotted after her. The two dogs jumped in and settled down on the towel spread along the bottom. Now Cody only had to wrangle the bulldog.

His mom lifted the soft-sided cooler from the ground. "Scoot over doggies. Make room for this."

She pushed Tyrus aside until she had enough space for the cooler. The two dogs snuggled up even closer.

His mother shook her head. "Two peas in a pod," she said. She began pulling the wagon behind her. "You got Bruno?"

"Yeah," Cody said. The bulldog tugged on his leash, wanting to run ahead, but Cody kept him in check.

"I'm not quite sure where to go from here," she said. "The locals know exactly what to do, but there aren't any signs directing people who just want to watch."

Melody nodded. "We'll do much better than this. Particularly if we want to advertise as far as Branson, maybe."

"Now that's something," his mother said. "Imagine people driving from Branson to come to our pet parade."

Several more cars pulled up and families piled out, some with dogs in tow. The three of them hesitated, waiting to see which way the others would go. When they started up the sidewalk, his mother followed with the wagon.

The route became obvious pretty quickly. Although it seemed Main Street would be the natural location of the parade, as they crossed the numbered streets and arrived at Third, the amount of activity intensified. Children sat along the sidewalks eating popsicles. Cones blocked off all the parking spots to avoid cars getting in the way. Vendors selling ice cream and water bottles and cotton candy walked along the street.

"Now we've found it," his mother said.

A gray-haired woman wearing a parade route T-shirt walked up to them. "Are you guys in the parade? The staging area is four blocks that way."

"Oh, no, we're just here to watch," Mom said.

"Nonsense. You've got pets and a wagon. You should be in it."

His mother glanced at the two of them. "What do you think?" She lowered her voice. "Should we infiltrate their event?"

Melody's laughter pealed, and then she snorted, covering her nose.

Cody couldn't stop himself from laughing at that. "Don't make Melody snort-laugh," he said. "We're not secret ops."

His mother waved at the woman, who had wandered toward another family trying to tame two Labrador puppies. "Hello! Can you tell me how long the parade route is?"

The woman turned back around to them. "About a mile."

His mother frowned. "What do you think, Cody? You up for a mile walk? Plus, I guess, whatever it takes to get back?"

Now she'd put him on the spot. Did he really want to walk in front of strangers with his walking stick and his clumsy gait?

But Melody leaned into the two of them conspiratorially. "We can't *all* be in the parade. Some of us have to actually be among the people to spy. Delilah, why don't you take Bruno and walk around the staging area to see what you can learn about the setup and how many people are needed to organize it? Cody and I will station ourselves along the parade route with our dogs and see what it's like to be on the perimeter."

Delilah nodded. "Smart thinking. If we're all in the same place, we won't know what's happening everywhere."

"Exactly," Melody said.

"How did we make it a day without you?" Delilah asked.

"I have no idea."

Everyone laughed, and Delilah walked off with Bruno toward the staging area.

"Nice work," Cody said. "You're good at ditching chaperones." He'd also neatly avoided having to lumber down a mile of hot streets with onlookers.

Melody grabbed the handle of the wagon and began tugging it the other direction. "I know how to get rid of nosy moms. I have a bazillion teenage girls who show me the ropes."

They walked along the parade route, which quickly filling with townspeople.

"Where do you think we should go?" she asked.

"It's thinner over here, so we shouldn't go too far or we might get away from the vendors," he said.

"How about here? I think we can see most of the street from this position." She pointed at a stretch of sidewalk in between two families where there was enough room for them and the wagon.

"Looks good to me."

The two of them wrangled the wagon into position and sat on the curb. An elderly man pushing an ice cream cart approached their side of the street.

Cody caught Melody looking at the cart rather longingly and pushed on his cane to get back to his feet. "I, for one, don't think a pet parade would be complete without ice cream," he said. "I'm going to go grab one. What can I get you?"

She looked like she was about to refuse, so he quickly added, "I know you're a good southern girl who won't make me eat ice cream alone."

She relented. "Anything chocolate. I would die for something chocolate right now."

"Done. Tend to the lovebirds," he said, glancing at the two dogs. "I'll be right back."

He bought two chocolate-dipped ice cream cones, and only when he accepted them both from the vendor did he realize how hard it was going to be to walk them over to Melody with his cane.

The man quickly noticed his situation and said, "I walk with a cane myself. That's why pushing a cart is so useful."

He demonstrated how Cody could easily manage both cones in one hand. "That should do it."

"Trick of the trade," Cody said. "Thank you."

Cody made his way back to Melody just as the sound of a marching band fired up several blocks away. The parade was about to begin.

Melody watched him return with a big smile. "Those two cones look delicious! Where's yours?"

He laughed as he dropped down beside her and passed one of the cones. "There's always more where those came from."

Both puppy dogs leaned their heads out of the wagon to sniff at the ice cream. "I guess I should get them some treats," Melody said.

"Good call. They might sneak attack us if we don't."

As Melody fed each of the dogs a biscuit from the cooler, the marching band appeared down the street. The townspeople began to clap along.

"Oh no," Melody said. "I can't clap with a cone in my hand!"

"I think the good people of Galena, Missouri, will understand," Cody said.

She leaned in closer, as the noise grew louder. He caught a whiff of her floral shampoo. "Do you think we could convince the band director to bring the marching band to our parade?"

"We can try. Since it wasn't planned before school let out, it might be hard to get them organized."

"He might be out of town himself, too," she said. "But it doesn't hurt to ask."

"Certainly."

Directly after the marching band was a truck pulling a trailer, similar to the one they'd seen earlier. A bunch of girls in matching uniforms stood on it, shaking their pom-poms to the band's music.

Now Cody leaned into Melody. "I guess that used to be you," he said.

"Back in the day." Her eyes followed the cheerleader float as it passed by.

"You miss it?"

"Sponsoring the pep squad helps," she said.

The music began to fade, making it easier to talk again. "So why aren't you the cheerleading coach?"

"Oh, Marjorie has been doing that for ages. I don't think she'll give it up any time soon."

"Could you assist her or something?"

"I do sometimes. But she seems to have it under control." Melody bit her lip, and Cody figured it was time for him to stop asking questions. Maybe being a cheerleading coach was her dream job, and thinking about how she hadn't accomplished it yet made her unhappy. He knew all about that.

She elbowed him. "Pay attention to this." She pulled out her phone.

A pickup truck rolled by, a huge sign on its bumper announcing the official pet store of Galena. The man driving the truck waved. In the back, two women flung little packages into the crowd. One landed at Melody's feet. She picked it up.

Cody leaned in again, using any excuse to close the distance between them. "What is it?"

"It's adorable," Melody said. The package had a sticker on the outside that read, "A treat for you and another for your pet." It listed the same pet store as the truck's banner.

"What's inside?"

"Two dog biscuits and a piece of candy," Melody said. "But both are just your standard prepackaged stuff, not fresh."

"Mom can top that, easy."

"Easy." They grinned at each other.

An old pickup truck—a 1950s Ford by the looks of it —rumbled past. In the back, a bunch of little kids tossed bead necklaces like it was Mardi Gras.

"Hmmm," Melody said. "I think everything should be pet related. Or candy for the kids."

"We can make that a requirement," Cody said. Melody snapped pictures of everything. A few more cars went by, convertibles with their tops down. Most carried hand-lettered signs for the businesses in town they represented.

Then the chorus of barking began.

"Let's grab the leashes just in case," Cody said.

They each reached into the wagon at the same time, and their hands brushed against each other.

Cody felt a little jolt at the accidental contact. He couldn't remember feeling this strongly about a girl before.

As the onslaught of barking, sniffing, yipping dogs approached, Tyrus remained calm and settled in the wagon.

Mistletoe? Not so much.

The Pomeranian leaped from the wagon, abandoning her soul mate, and streaked out into the street

Melody pulled back on her leash. "Mistletoe! No!" She reeled the line back in.

Mistletoe had gone full Tasmanian Devil, barking herself in tight circles, her sandy fur puffed out like an angry cat.

"Mistletoe! Stop!" Melody cried and pulled her into her lap. Mistletoe scrabbled, trying to break away.

The dogs and their owners, old and young, eventually passed. Some dragged their dogs along. Others seemed to be dragged *by* them. A few carried their quaking pups. Cody spotted his mother and lifted his arm in a wave. She beamed back at him and gave a big thumbs up sign.

"She's having a good time," Melody said, still trying to hang onto the wildly yapping Mistletoe.

The parade closed with a police car. Galena didn't have its own force, it seemed, so it was a Missouri State Highway Patrol car with its lights on that completed the lineup.

When it passed, people began to wander the empty street.

The vendors took up their cries with renewed fervor. Ice cream! Dog toys! Foam rockets! Bottled water!

Melody was completely frazzled over Mistletoe. "I can't believe the way she acted."

"It was a lot of dogs to deal with. I'm sure quite a few dropped out of the parade as soon as they approached the mob at the starting point."

Mistletoe had not completely settled, still occasionally jumping out to snap at a passing dog.

"Put her back in with Tyrus," Cody said. "Maybe he can do something with her."

And he was right. As soon as the Pomeranian was back in the wagon, Tyrus stood and shifted his legs so that he stood over the ball of brown fluff.

Mistletoe immediately settled, lying down on the

bottom of the wagon, staunchly protected by the retriever.

"See?" Cody said. "She doesn't feel as vulnerable."

"Look at that." Melody stood up. "I guess it's safe enough to go find your mom if you're ready."

"Sure." Cody braced himself on his stick to stand up again. "Then maybe we can offload the granddogs and see what there is to see in this town."

It was a little bit of a risky thing to say, to suggest that they were a couple and their dogs had a relationship with his mother.

But when Melody gave him a big smile, like he had just said the cleverest thing, he started to relax. Maybe he was more than the boss's son, someone to stay on the good side of. Maybe, on a complete whim of fate, he had found someone he could be around without feeling miserable or incomplete.

In fact, this whole day had put him on top of the world. He felt motivated in a way he never had before.

He felt like he could do anything.

Melody liked being around him. And they were going to put on a pet parade together in July.

So he was going to be in it.

Not watching from the sidelines. But taking part, strolling right down the big middle.

Without a walking stick.

CHAPTER 13

*T*he day after the parade, Melody's visit with her grandmother was full of questions. "I see that gleam in your eye," Grandma said. "Tell me about the boy. What's happened?"

"We went to a parade in a small town called Galena yesterday," Melody said.

"Did you have a good time?"

"We did. All the things I worried about going into it turned out not to matter at all."

Grandma patted Melody's knee. "That's often the way of it. The sooner you learn it, the happier life will be."

"We had ice cream and watched the dogs. We were just like any ordinary couple."

"Why wouldn't you be?"

Melody hesitated. She didn't really want to burden Grandma with any of the harder aspects of her relationship with Cody.

"Come on, now. Troubles shared are troubles halved."

Melody rested her hand on Mistletoe, who lay between them as usual. "He served in the military."

"Well, what a fine thing." Grandma's brows knitted in concern. "Did something happen to him there?"

Melody nodded. "He walks with a cane. I get a sense that he was pretty injured, although we've never talked about exactly what happened."

"You should. Get it out in the open."

"I can try. Everything feels so new and tender."

"It's early yet. Give it time."

"His moods shift a lot," Melody said, getting to the real heart of the matter. "He can be dark and brooding one day, and light and easy going the next."

"Now I see. So you spend a lot of time worrying if his change of mood has something to do with you."

"Yes. But also it just worries me in general. Like I never know what to expect."

"Well, I'm not going to give you the bad piece of advice that love conquers all. It's time and safety, and a regular dose of happiness that does it."

"I think we definitely meet that criteria already," Melody said.

"Then you're halfway there."

They chatted for a little while, then, all too soon, a staff worker came out to take her grandmother back inside.

"Why are our visits so short now?" Melody asked.

"Layla is on a medication that limits her sun exposure," the woman said kindly. "But she likes it out here in the gardens with you and your dog."

"You mean I could talk to her more if we were inside?" Melody asked.

"Certainly," the woman said.

Grandma looked down at her hands folded in her lap.

"Why didn't you tell me?" Melody asked.

"Because I know how much you love to bring Mistletoe. I love seeing her."

Melody felt her indignation rise. "How do we get permission to bring Mistletoe inside?" she asked, panic threatening to consume her. "I can't do anything about her now, but I can leave her at home until it's done. Is there paperwork?"

Grandma reached out to squeeze Melody's hand. "Don't you fret, sweet girl. I like the sunshine."

"But I like spending more time with you!" Melody felt as though the sky were darkening and storm clouds rolling in.

"Only service dogs are allowed inside the building," the woman said kindly. "You can imagine how crazy it would be if everyone brought in the beloved dogs of residents."

Melody could see that. But a service dog. What did that entail? Could Mistletoe become one? Was that even a reasonable thought for a Pomeranian? She would have to look it up.

"Did you bring the box?" Grandma asked the woman.

"I did." She passed a small cardboard cube to Grandma.

"This is for you, my girl."

Melody managed to settle herself enough to pay attention to the gift. "What is it?"

"You'll see."

The box wasn't wrapped, so Melody untucked the flap to peer inside. Red tissue paper obscured whatever it might be.

She reached in and felt something cool and round.

She lifted it out. It was a Christmas ornament, clear pale-green glass hand-painted with a Christmas tree, two small presents, and a fluffy dog asleep beneath the bows.

"Grandma, it's beautiful. Did you paint this?"

"I was having a less shaky day," Grandma said. "I was never a great artist, but I could render a scene when I wanted to."

Melody held the glass bulb by its green ribbon and turned it around. On the backside, near the base of the sphere, her grandmother had signed it simply *Layla*.

"I will cherish it," Melody said. "Was this part of your Christmas in July?"

"It was," Grandma said. "I'm glad to get one more ornament on your tree."

"Well, I have every intention of springing you from here in December so that you can put it on my tree yourself," she said. She looked up at the staff worker, who was reaching for Grandma's hand to help her off the bench. "You guys do let them go for the day on Christmas, right?"

"We do," she said. "For all the residents who are well enough."

She qualified for it. Her grandmother turned to the woman. "Did you know Christmas is my favorite holiday?"

"Then I'm sure you're excited about our Christmas in July," she said.

"Absolutely," her grandmother said as she slowly eased to standing. "I'll take as much Christmas as I can get."

Melody hugged her grandmother fiercely, then waited until she had disappeared inside the building.

What medicine was Grandma taking that kept her out of the sun? And why was she deteriorating so fast now, going from lengthy visits to one-hour visits to being helped to stand in just a few weeks?

Melody would pore over the reports and try to figure it out. But in the meantime, she would look into service dog certification. And figure out how to get more Christmas for Grandma.

When Cody arrived at the expansion Monday morning, the freshly painted room smelled not only of the renovation, but also of warm baked goods. With the door open between the two stores, the space was beginning to feel a lot more like the extension of the bakery it would eventually become.

Cody no more settled Tyrus in his big, round bed when his mother entered the back room. "I've been thinking nonstop about that pet parade," she said. "Fred said he would talk to Officer Stone about any permits we might need to close off Town Square. Because of the way Applebottom is set up, we could easily start at the far end of Main, march right up to Town Square, take the road in the circle, and then have all of the vendors and tents and things set up around the gazebo in the center."

Cody nodded. "That's definitely something they didn't have in Galena. It was a straight line, so the vendors had to be mobile. We could definitely have a big event ready for all the walkers and their pets when they got to the Square."

Delilah clapped her hands. "This is too perfect."

"Let me go open the front door for Melody," he said. "I'll be right back."

His legs were warm and pliant with the workout he'd already done early that morning. He'd definitely stepped things up and spent time walking last night. He didn't exactly expect to improve overnight, not after so much therapy already, but he realized that the last bit of magic had been missing. And he had it now. Motivation.

When he opened the door, he was surprised to see the Melody was already there. And today, she had brought Mistletoe with her.

He'd barely gotten the door open when Melody barged in.

"I have so many ideas, I have to tell you them all before they disappear."

"Okay," Cody said with a chuckle. "Good morning to you, too."

Melody held up a hand. "No time for Applebottom pleasantries. I need to figure out how to get Mistletoe trained to be a service dog. And I have an idea for the pet parade."

His mother stepped into the room from the back. "Why, hello, Melody," she said. "How are you today?"

"She doesn't have time for Applebottom pleasantries, Mom," he said with another chuckle.

Melody put her hands on her hips and tried to give him the evil eye, but it was way too adorable to be effective. A surge of conflicting emotions flowed through him. He liked her. In fact, he was starting to more than like her. It was almost time to take the risk and ask her to do something, just the two of them. They'd really already done it on Saturday. It was just a matter of making it official. Something his mother hadn't suggested first.

He'd give himself another week or two. What if he could go on a date without the cane?

He pictured them walking along the lake in Branson, stopping for packets of baked fish or a bit of cake. A life like he had once imagined.

"Well, what is it?" his mom asked.

Melody's face was flushed. She pulled back on Mistletoe, who was trying to make her way to the back area where she had sniffed out the location of Tyrus.

"Fine," Melody said. "Go on." She dropped the end of the leash.

Mistletoe tore through the room into the back.

"Those star-crossed lovers," his mom said.

"Instead of just being a pet parade," Melody said. "Why don't we do a Christmas theme?"

"In July?" Cody asked.

Melody shot him a look.

He held up his hands. "I'm just asking. You do mean in July right?"

"Yes. Christmas in July is a thing." Melody seemed indignant that he didn't know.

"It is," his mother said.

"We could have a contest for the cutest pet costume," Melody said. "People who might not get out to watch a bunch of people walking their dogs might come to see dogs dressed up as cute elves or Santa."

"I like it," Delilah. "What gave you this brainstorm?"

"My grandmother," she said. She finally paused, her rapid unspooling of thoughts seeming to come to an end. "She said that sometimes when people knew they weren't going to make it to Christmas, it was nice to give them one last chance to see the wonder and the lights."

Her voice broke a little at the end, and his mother rushed forward to envelop Melody in a hug. "Oh, my sweet girl. Will your grandmother be able to come to our Christmas pet parade?"

"I'm going to try. She's on the chemotherapy medication that means she can't be out in the sun much. And it *is* summer."

"Then we will just have to construct the grandest, most comfortable, most sun-defying float ever for

Grandma," his mother said. "We'll shade her and get a fan on her. Provide a nice cushy chair."

Cody could only watch the two women as they hugged and commiserated. Cody had lost both his grandmothers years ago.

His mother stepped back, squeezing Melody's hand. "In fact, if you want to do this, we might as well do it right. We'll get as many trailers as we can. We could affix some tent covers for shade. I'm sure Cody here could wire the fans. And we could invite a bunch of the residents at the Applebottom nursing home here. Where is your grandma, dear?"

"She's about an hour away, at Brookdale."

"I can put the word out to them, too. Their social worker could find some residents who are fit to make the journey and the parade."

Cody remained by the door, his hand on his walking stick. Something had just happened here, and the emotion in the room permeated them all.

But he had one more thought to add.

"I bet some of those citizens had pets they had to leave behind with family when they moved to a nursing home. We should make sure they know that they can bring them to sit with them on the float. We can station a volunteer or two on each trailer to help, in case some of the animals are wild."

"We can leash them down so they don't jump off." His mom beamed at Melody. "This is an amazing idea. A beautiful idea. The Christmas in July Pet Parade, honoring the seasoned members of our communities."

She released Melody and headed for the bakery

door. "I'll talk to the girl who does all my ads," she said. "We'll come up with something snazzy for the posters and the signs around town. Maybe we'll even put something in the Branson newspaper. I bet we could get a reporter to come out."

She was mostly talking to herself now, continuing the conversation even as she left the room.

Melody and Cody looked at each other and laughed.

"It really is a great idea," Cody said.

"You think so? I was worried that it was too self-serving."

"Are you kidding me? It's serving everybody."

More than anything, Cody wanted to put his arms around Melody and draw her close. But they weren't there yet. Before he could lay any claim on her, he had to actually ask her out.

And for that, he wanted to walk on two good legs.

CHAPTER 14

That night, Cody took to his computer to find out what rehab specialists might be available near him. There were none in Applebottom itself, but there were several in nearby Branson. His hopes ran high, imagining that he could meet with them, and with his renewed eagerness to work—and not feeling buried under the stifling anxiety of PTSD—he would improve rapidly.

But his hopes were quickly dashed, as every website he visited talked about waiting lists or difficulties with certain types of insurance.

Cody slammed his hand on the dining room table with frustration. Tyrus immediately popped up from where he lay in his bed a few feet away, pressing his head against Cody's thigh.

Cody reached down to pet the dog. "I'm okay, Tyrus. Just frustrated, that's all."

Tyrus was not convinced, however, and gripped the bottom edge of Cody's shorts with his teeth to pull him away from the computer. Cody started to laugh. "Puppy dog, you're as bad as my mother."

Tyrus must've understood his tone, if not his words, because he gave an indignant *woof*. Cody allowed himself to be nudged across the room to the sofa.

"Are you trying to turn me into a couch potato?"

Another gentle *woof*.

Still, Cody sat there with the dog until Tyrus seemed reasonably assured that Cody was indeed calm.

"Surely, there has to be something," Cody said. He stood up and returned to his computer. This time, instead of typing in "rehabilitation," he tried "physical therapy."

A new name came up. A woman from Applebottom who worked in the schools. Cody knew her. She was the one who did his nephew William's therapy. She apparently took on private patients over the summer, self-pay only. He reviewed her rates. Unlike the big-name treatment centers, she was quite reasonable.

He could do that. He filled out her new patient form, and after it was sent, stared at her name as if it was his future.

Ginny Page.

Cody chose Thursday of that week as his first day to work with Ginny. Melody wouldn't be in the shop that day. She was meeting some friend of hers, so she wouldn't notice his absence.

His optimism that the rehabilitation would work this time was so high it affected everything, even the way he interacted with Melody. In fact, on the Wednesday before his first session, he surprised Melody with a little gift.

The cake decorator from Tea for Two had come over to work with his mother on some of the special dog treats they would be showing off at the grand opening.

After Melody had left, he headed over to say goodbye to his mother to discover the decorator was drawing various dog faces on big, round cookie treats.

"Look at this," his mother said, holding up a perfect rendition of Bruno, her bulldog. "We have a Labrador and a poodle."

Cody looked them over. "Could you do a light-brown Pomeranian?" he asked Sandy.

"Certainly," she said. "Where's the chicken paste?"

His mother passed a pale tube to Sandy.

Cody had only run into the decorator once or twice since returning to Applebottom. He knew that she was a long-time resident, but she'd moved to the outskirts of town when he was still a boy.

She was quite the talk of the town, though, a decorator with some pretty serious credentials, including the New York Met Gala. Even so, she primarily worked in Applebottom.

She quickly outlined the face of a Pomeranian—nose uplifted—and added little squiggles to show the fluffiness of the hair.

She switched to a darker paste and filled in the eyes

and nose. Then a pink one made of pork created a tiny tongue.

"Is this for a particular dog owner?" Sandy asked.

His mother smiled at him knowingly as he said, "The dog's name is Mistletoe."

While Sandy added the name underneath the head of the dog, his mother opened the drawer and pulled out a clear cellophane treat bag.

Melody loved it.

"It's so precious!" she cried. She threw her arms around his neck in a close, tight hug.

Both Tyrus and Mistletoe lifted their heads from where they lay together to watch.

Cody set his cane against the wall, wrapping both his arms around her.

She smelled of paint, caulking, and floral shampoo.

She was slight, and his hands easily reached his own elbows as they came around her.

She felt perfect in his arms, and he wondered how long they could stay there before it became more than a friendly hug.

But she held it, seeming to appreciate the feel of him, too. They breathed together for just a moment, then, at last, Melody dropped down from her tiptoes, and he released her.

"I can't possibly let Mistletoe eat it," she said, gazing at it again through the clear cellophane.

"I guess you could freeze it for a while," he said.

"Freeze it forever!" Her eyes shined, and he washed over with the warm feeling of having pleased her.

"I'll miss you tomorrow," he said, then worried that it was too much, too fast.

But Melody simply said, "I'll miss you, too. It's just one day, though. Surely we can make it till Friday." Her sparkly eyes teased him, and he was glad she was able to make the moment less awkward.

She was definitely the prettiest thing he had ever laid eyes on. Had he really just held her in his arms, even as a thank you? It seemed impossible.

"Friday, then," he said.

She patted her knees, and when Mistletoe declined to leave Tyrus aside, stomped over to them with her hands on her hips. "Mistletoe Hopkins, you come with me right now. You'll see Tyrus again on Friday."

For a moment, Cody flashed with the vision of Melody, her hands on her hips, gently scolding a little boy for tracking mud through her house. Their house.

The boy in his head was the spitting image of himself as a kid, and when the little guy poked out his lips in upset, Melody scooped him up to squeeze him to her cheek. The image was as clear to him as the scene in the shop.

He had to shake it away. He'd never seen the future quite so clearly, almost as vivid as the terrible flashbacks that plagued him. In fact, since his injury, he hadn't pictured a future like that at all.

Melody waved a hand in front of his face. "Earth to Cody," she said. "You still in there?"

"Still here," he said. He slapped his thigh as well. "Come along Tyrus. Time to go home."

He picked up his cane and walked Melody and Mistletoe to the front door. "Until Friday," he said.

She paused by the door. "Thank you again for the dog cookie."

They held their positions for a moment, breathlessly close. He could have easily leaned down just a few inches and kissed her.

But then she was gone, walking Mistletoe out into the bright late afternoon sunshine.

As Cody locked the door, he could barely contain the happy feeling growing in his chest.

This was all going to work out. The new physical therapy. The pet store. Melody. All of it. He just had to get started.

CHAPTER 15

On Thursday morning, Melody set out for the drive up to Springfield to see one of her old cheerleading friends from college. Nova had just gotten married and was passing through with her new husband on their way to California, where he was starting a new job and they would be setting up their first home.

Melody and Nova had been friends since freshman year of college, when they both made the cheerleading squad and ended up living across the hall from each other in the athletic dorm. Nova had been one of Melody's roommates when they'd gotten the house so that Melody could bring Mistletoe with her.

"You're going to be so happy to see her again," Melody said to Mistletoe, who snoozed off and on in her carrier strapped to the front seat.

Nova had texted her that she'd found an outdoor café where Mistletoe could hang out with them as they had lunch. Melody punched the address in her phone and navigated to a little row of shops on the north side.

As Melody approached the tables, she recognized her friend immediately.

Nova was truly beautiful with deep ebony skin and warm bright eyes. She'd traded her long curling extensions for tight braids rolled into adorable little balls on either side of her head, but it didn't matter that her hairstyle had changed so drastically. Melody would know her anywhere.

The two of them moved together for a tight hug.

"It's Mistletoe!" Nova squealed. She bent down to scoop up the little dog. "She's still so precious!"

"How was the wedding?" Melody asked.

"Glorious. I'm telling you, if you can get away with it, a destination wedding is the way to go." Nova sat down at a small, round table already outfitted with two glasses of water and a set of menus.

"Tell me all about it," Melody said.

And Nova did, how only their parents and siblings had been invited, and the waves had lapped at the shore. The officiant had been barefoot. And afterward, they had walked out in the water for pictures, the others lifting the hem of her dress so it wouldn't get wet.

By then, the waitress had come for the order and Mistletoe was snoozing under the table.

"What about you?" Nova asked. "Anything in the romance front?"

Melody hesitated. Did she mention Cody? Was something going on there? "Well..."

"I knew it!" Nova said. "I could smell it!" She leaned

in. "Tell me everything. Every scintillating detail."

It was nice to talk about Cody to someone. While there were a lot of people in Applebottom that Melody enjoyed being around as coworkers and neighbors, she didn't feel like she had a close girlfriend nearby anymore. Certainly not like Nova, or her other roommates from college.

"He's ex-military," Melody began. "He's from the small town where I work now, but he was gone several years during his service."

"I like it," Nova said. "Go on."

"He's incredibly handsome, in an edgy way. But he's really sweet. At least to me."

"Edgy but sweet. Check."

His family owns a pet store that they are expanding, so this summer I've been helping them get it ready."

Now Nova held up a hand. "Wait. So you took an extra job for the summer?"

"Yeah. I can always use the extra cash." Melody took a sip of water to avoid saying more. She didn't want to get into the issues with her grandmother and the bills that she faced.

"So true," Nova said. "I'm not sure we will ever pay off this wedding trip."

"Cody has been doing the construction part, and I've been painting. So it's a lot of time together."

"Excellent. So what's the deal? Have you been going out? Is he getting serious?"

"Maybe? It hasn't been very long. Just a couple of weeks. But he does all these sweet things for me. I don't know."

Nova sat back in her chair. Every time she moved, half the people sitting outside turned to look at her again. She was that beautiful. Everyone had been surprised when she'd given up cheerleading because she had been a shoo-in for a pro team. She was the sort of girl you could picture in a magazine. But she never seemed to notice, or care, and had taken a job in business.

"Do you *want* it to get serious?"

"I think so! But we have a long way to go."

"Well, it's a promising start. You have to keep me updated." She glanced behind Melody. "There's Adam!" She waved frantically for him to come over. "I can't wait for you to meet him. It feels so strange to be married to someone my best friend's never even got to meet."

Adam approached and plunked down in a chair. "I don't want to interrupt the girl talk." He said with a smile. "Nova talks so much about you."

"I've missed her," Melody said.

"At least we're on the same continent again," Nova said.

After that, the conversation centered on Adam's new job, and how the two of them met in France where they'd worked at the same company. They had only dated six months before getting married, but looking at the two of them, they seemed very happy.

Melody felt a twinge of jealousy. She wanted this, too. Small towns made it difficult. But maybe, just maybe, things were working out with Cody. She did like him. They should probably do something away from Applebottom soon. She wouldn't blame him if he waited until this job was done, though. It was smart, really, in case it didn't work out in the end. Might be miserable painting next to each other in awkward silence.

Maybe by the next time she caught up with Nova, she would have more of a story to tell.

❧

Melody still had Nova on her mind when she arrived at the pet store expansion the next day. When Cody opened the door, she noticed that he looked a little different. Strained, maybe. Definitely more dark and brooding than she had seen in a while.

Mistletoe raced to the back room to find Tyrus, then stopped short when she realized Tyrus was right behind the door with Cody. The retriever seemed to know something was up as well, because even before Cody could step forward to shut the door, Tyrus was right there, making every move with his master.

"Everything okay?" Melody asked.

"I'm fine," Cody grumbled. Tyrus shifted beneath Cody's hand again.

Mistletoe tried to stand beneath the retriever's chest as she often did. But today, Tyrus was clearly fully on duty. He sidestepped the little Pomeranian, carefully keeping pace with his master.

Melody set her backpack in the corner. Something was definitely wrong. She watched Cody limp painfully to the newly constructed counter. He could barely stagger there.

She hurried to see if she could be of help, but he held out his hand to stop her. "I'm fine," he said again, but his tone could have shaken the leaves off a tree.

Melody didn't know him well enough to get him to talk about whatever was going on. She opened her mouth to say something bright and encouraging out of habit, but then closed it again.

Cody didn't need small talk or clichés. He needed space.

He circled behind the counter and lowered himself down onto the stool. He bent over to screw in the hardware to the drawers on the backside, the knobs and locks scattered across the top.

Originally, they had planned for her to paint the counter today, but as he sat there with one hand splayed on its surface for balance, she decided not to mention it.

Until she figured out how to approach him in his current state, Melody would simply have to find some other work to do.

She went into the public bathroom and took her time getting the difficult bits around the tile and mirror clean and crisp. But eventually, the work there was done, and she had to move out to the main shop.

Cody was nowhere to be seen. Was he in the back? Should she follow him? Find him?

He was in pain, she decided. She remembered when Nova had gotten injured during the third game of their junior year. She'd been devastated, not just because of the injury. But the fear. She just knew she was going to get cut from the squad, an alternate taking her place.

She'd been grouchy to pretty much everybody,

including Melody. But she eventually got past it. And so would Cody. Melody could wait.

She opened the paint cans of smooth enamel that would cover the top of the counter. This would be difficult, careful work to avoid bubbles or imperfections right where the customer would be standing.

She threw herself into the job, not even noticing the time until Delilah passed through the doorway between the shops. She held two plastic containers.

"Lunch!" She glanced around. "Where's Cody?"

"He was here earlier, but I haven't seen him for a while."

Melody focused back in on the last section of the counter. For once, she was thankful that Cody's mother was so close. She could go in search of her son instead of Melody.

Delilah headed to the back and greeted her son.

Melody finished the last bit slowly and carefully, then stuck her brush in the tray. What was going on back there?

Their voices were a low murmur. Then gradually a little louder. "It's fine," she heard Cody say. "Just take hers."

When Delilah returned, her face was etched with concern. "Here is your lunch," she said. "Feel free to take it wherever you want to eat."

Melody desperately wanted to ask Delilah what was going on, what she knew, but she simply nodded. Delilah almost set the container on the bright, wet paint, but caught herself just in time. "Oh! That would've been a disaster."

Melody accepted the box. "Thank you so much for providing lunch."

"It's been my pleasure." Delilah glanced around. "I think the painting is almost done, isn't it?"

"Yes, unless you want me to paint the back room. The walls are done. I finished the bathroom this morning. There's just this counter trim work, and then anything you might want me to do on the shelving once it's up."

"I think I'm just going to leave them silver," Delilah said, looking around. "I should have the stencils for the paw prints tomorrow. Do you think that will be your last day?"

"Unless you want me to scrape the windows. I'm happy to do that, too."

Delilah turned to the front. "That's right. The windows." She hesitated. "Let me talk to Cody about that." She flashed a sad smile. "On a different day."

She left for the bakery without another word.

Great. Now what? Melody set the lunch box on the floor, remembered the dogs, and picked it back up again. She walked it over to a ladder to rest on a high step, then returned to the counter, checking the edges and seams. It was all done. It looked really good.

She cleaned off the brush and closed the paint can. She definitely had to come back tomorrow to put up the paw prints, but maybe she was just done for the day. Maybe she was nearly finished with the job.

She couldn't let things end like this. She picked up her lunch container again and headed to the back. She had to find her dog anyway.

"Mistletoe?" she called as she passed through the doorway.

Her dog lay alone in Tyrus's big dog bed. Cody sat on the stool in the corner, screwing together shelving. Tyrus stood right by his feet.

"There you are," Melody said. "Did you want to have lunch?"

He ignored her.

Melody stood there in the center of the room, holding her lunch box and waiting. She had no clue what to do.

Cody continued to work on the shelf as if she wasn't there.

She could take Mistletoe and just sneak out.

But that wasn't her way. She and Cody had been getting along amazingly, right up until this morning. What happened yesterday while they were apart?

She approached him so quietly that when she said, "How are the shelves coming?" he jumped on the stool.

"They're fine," he said quickly.

Tyrus let out a little *woof.* Cody reached down to pet his head. "I'm okay, boy."

"You sure?" Melody asked. "He's not leaving your side."

Cody's jaw set more firmly, as if he was trying to control himself. Was he mad at her?

"Did I do something wrong?" she asked. "We haven't spoken all day. I thought we were getting along so well."

At that, Cody stopped screwing a brace onto a shelf. "You didn't do anything wrong," he said.

"Then can we just have lunch together?" This was

the farthest out on a limb she had gone since they met. Her stomach quaked at how he might respond.

He gripped the screwdriver so tightly his knuckles turned white. But then he said, "Okay."

Melody let out a gentle sigh of relief that this had worked out. "Shall I pull up a piece of tarp? We can stay here."

"That would probably be best," he said.

Melody hurried to the corner to grab one of the unused canvas tarps, an extra they had never unfolded. She spread it on the floor, scooting aside a couple of boxes to make room. She no more sat down when Mistletoe hurried over to sniff at the box.

"This isn't for you," she said to the dog, petting her head.

Cody was slow to pick up his cane and the plastic container and make his way to the tarp. Tyrus never got more than a few inches from his side.

He tried to bend down to place the plastic container on the ground, but he couldn't seem to get close enough without dropping it.

"I got it," Melody said. "It's tough being so darn tall."

He grunted at that and passed her the box.

He bent his left leg, his injured one curiously straight today. But something in the way he had to move didn't work out as he expected, and he half fell, half collapsed onto the floor.

"Oh!" she said. "Are you okay?"

"Just stop it," he said. "Stop fawning over me."

Melody sat back. This was proving to be a terribly

unpleasant lunch. Cody adjusted himself onto the floor and the two of them ate in silence.

The sandwiches, the same ones that she and Cody had picked out at their first lunch of Tea for Two, tasted like sawdust today. She forced herself to eat them, but, as the silence lingered, she didn't know where they could go from here.

Would there always be days like this? How often did they come? What caused them?

"So I finished the counter," she said, unable to stand the silence a moment more. "The bathroom, too. I think I might be done until I get the paw print stencil, which your mother said would come tomorrow. She wanted them to match her van."

He nodded at her, and it was easier than the silence so she rattled on, spouting details about how the countertop had gone smoothly and how well put together it was, on and on and on. Cody never responded in any way.

Eventually, they finished their lunch but continued to sit there.

"It sounds like the parade is really coming together," Melody said. "I was in the pie shop, and Maude told me that they were going to have a booth. And some pet groomer from Branson was going to come in. And someone with the pet sitting company. I think they even convinced one of the dog food companies to send a representative."

Cody sat on the floor, his gaze still focused on his empty carton.

Melody truly didn't know what to do. She decided

to drop the Manic Pixie Dream Girl attitude and get a little more real.

She reached out her hand to cup over Cody's arm. "I know I'm really talkative. It's how I fill up a space. I'm just worried about you."

He did finally turn his head toward her then. "I know."

Well, that was something.

"Are you sure there's nothing I can do? I assume it's your leg. I'm not good at amputations, but I know how to work a saw."

Now he grunted out a laugh. "Thanks."

Her shoulders relaxed. She had done it. Gotten him back.

"I just did some extra workouts," he said. "It didn't go well."

"I sort of know what you mean. When I was a cheerleader..." She hesitated. "I know that sounds ridiculous when I say it out loud. *Cheerleader.* But when I was in the athletic department in college, I really needed to learn this new maneuver for a routine. The woman doing the choreography didn't like several of us, nobody knew why. So she created this dance that was pretty much impossible. I was determined to do it. But it required me to be stronger."

Now she had his attention.

"What was it?" he asked.

"Instead of simply being lifted into the air, where I mostly have to keep my balance, this one I had to do a handstand on someone else's hands. It was really advanced. Probably a little unnecessary for what we did, but I was determined to do it. The problem was, to be stable in that position, I had to be really strong, not just in the arms but also in my core. I tripled my workouts to try to get stronger and better, and after one of those days of working out too much, I don't know if I tweaked something, or if I was just sore, but I literally could not bend in the middle."

"That sounds rough."

"It was. And that woman, I think she had pain radar. Because she kept having me do the most terrible things until I thought I was just going to scream. I'm quite sure I was literally the worst person to be around, and I stumbled and fell and was more clumsy than usual because I was trying to work around the pain. But I did get past it."

Cody looked down at the tarp. "It's a nice story," he said. "But I'm not a cheerleader. And this is not a difficult dance move. This is my life. My ability to even walk. And it's not working."

She shook her head. "That's where you're wrong, Cody. Maybe you did too much yesterday. Maybe tried something new and failed. You can't say after one day that it's not working. It's simply isn't working *yet*."

His expression was ragged, like he was wrecked inside. But he shifted on the floor to pet Tyrus. "All right," he said. "It isn't working *yet*."

"Let's hang some shelving," she said. "You be the brains and I'll be the brawn."

He laughed again, and after a bit of stumbling, arm clutching, and general clumsiness, they both got to their feet to work.

his was not what Cody wanted.

When Melody finally left for the day, all the shelving up on the walls of the new pet store, Cody knew he would not be back any time soon.

The work was mostly done. They had some cleanup in the back, and then to wait for supplies to come to be stocked. But until the first deliveries arrived, there was little else to do.

And he didn't want to be around Melody while he was starting this new therapy. Not after today.

He sat on the stool a long time, not just lost in thought, but frankly, unsure he could even lift himself up.

His mother shut down the bakery next door and came to check on him.

"Are you in a better mood than earlier?" she asked.

"I don't know." He didn't keep the darkness from his voice.

"Something get to you today?" She ran her hands

across the smooth counter. Melody really had done a perfect job.

"Nothing new," he said.

"We're all here to help."

"I know that."

"You need some company?"

"Not really."

"All right. I'm locking up the other side. You got this one?"

"I do."

His mother glanced around. "I'll start letting the goods get delivered now. Going to be showtime soon." She hesitated. "You think you're going to stay on and help with the shop or should I hire someone?"

"I don't know anything right now."

"That's all right," she said. "You have a good night."

After she had disappeared to the other side, and he had listened to her call Bruno to follow her out the back door, and even when it was locked up and everything had gone silent, still he sat there.

Everything hurt. He had to take care with painkillers because some of them interfered with the other medicine he took, the one for the nightmares. Generally, he just toughed it out.

But this was a whole new level of pain. He considered the work Ginny had put him through. Some of the exercises were similar to what he'd done before, but others were all new.

It wasn't working.

He remembered what Melody had said to him. It wasn't working *yet*.

She'd gotten him out of his funk, he'd give her that. But he knew a lot more about his condition than she did.

He felt his motivation starting to wane, and wondered how to lift it back up. This was where he'd always been, at least in the months since the explosion. Then, over the last week, he'd been as optimistic as he'd ever been in his life.

But that feeling was long gone now.

Tyrus sat near his feet. The evening was moving on and he should go. But instead, he pulled out his phone and called Ginny. He thought she might be in another session, but she answered the phone.

"Cody? You okay?" Her voice was no-nonsense, same as if she was telling him to do a one-legged squat or roll a medicine ball with his foot.

"I'm just experiencing a level of post-workout after-effects I've never seen before."

"I'm not surprised," she said. "It looked to me as if you've been favoring your strengths in your workouts, not actually forcing yourself to improve your weaknesses."

She had him there.

"I think you'll experience a couple of weeks of abject misery. After that, you should slowly pull out of it."

"What shot do I really have at getting better?"

She paused for a moment, and he half expected her to say, "None whatsoever."

But then she said, "There's always room for improvement. And, certainly, you don't want to regress. Do I think you're ever going to walk without a limp? I don't know about that. There's a lot of damage and pieces and parts that are just flat gone. Shortened ligaments. Missing muscle. But you can do better than you are. If your goal is to walk without a cane, I think that's possible. Not in the short term, but it's definitely possible."

"Are we back on tomorrow?"

"Back on tomorrow," she said. "Three times a week."

"All right. See you then."

He shoved his phone back into his pocket.

He wasn't sure exactly what he hoped for now. It looked as though he would land somewhere in between his aspirations and his current state.

But one thing was pretty clear to him. He needed to do this away from Melody. She might have been bubbly and helpful today, but he knew exactly what he was capable of if things got tough. And once he snuffed the light for him out of her eyes, he could be pretty sure it would never come back. He couldn't risk it.

So, no, he was not coming back to the pet store until he was ready.

§

When Melody arrived at the pet store the next morning, she wasn't completely surprised to see Delilah in the space instead of Cody.

Mistletoe took off for the back room with a little yelp, racing around and eventually returning to the two women, her head slung low.

"They're not here, darling," Delilah said to the dog.

She faked a smile at Melody. "Cody is taking a little break. But he will be here to help us with the pet parade. He wasn't really going to be able to unload stock and boxes easily anyway. Do you think you can help with that? Do you want to keep working here?"

More work meant more money. "Sure," Melody said. "Is it time to scrape the windows yet?"

Delilah looked around. "Let's put those paw prints up on the wall. And do you think you could stencil Nothing But a Pound Dog on the backside? Do you have good lettering skills?"

Melody smiled even though she didn't really feel like it. "Does a cheerleader have a megaphone?"

"I thought so. Once that's done, let's do the windows. There should be some large blades somewhere for that. I bought them early on."

"I'll find them," Melody said.

"After that, we'll move the hooks in the bakery with the dog toys in here. Then deliveries should start happening every day. And we'll get the signs in. We'll have to organize everything for the parade. It's a lot."

"I can do it."

"I bet you can."

Delilah was about to head back to the bakery, but Melody stopped her. "How is he, like really? He has seemed so fine."

Another false smile. "He has good days and bad days," Delilah said. "I'm not sure what happened yesterday."

"He was definitely not himself."

"It's the way he's been most of the time since his return."

Mistletoe approached Delilah to sniff at her bakery-scented hands. She smiled down at the little dog and pulled a treat from her pocket.

"But I will tell you one thing, in all the days he's been back, good or bad, there's definitely been one thing that has made him better."

"Really?" Melody asked. "What's that?"

"You."

CHAPTER 17

*C*ody had to acknowledge Ginny had been right about one thing. The next week was brutal.

She put him through the wringer, building on the exercises at every visit, and adding things for him to do from home every morning.

She hadn't seen his PTSD activate, but that changed after getting triggered a few days in when he tripped over a barbell on the floor and fell into the weight rack, sending the whole thing crashing over.

He'd gone into a full-blown rage, the sort he hadn't done since returning home.

But Ginny had been completely unflappable, approaching him carefully, starting him on breathing techniques, dimming the lights, and sending soothing aromatherapy through the room until he calmed.

Tyrus, too, had gotten involved, tugging at his shorts to move him away from the heavy weights.

After a long talk about his situation, Ginny had arranged for his old doctor at the VA hospital to prescribe something to get him through the hardest part of the therapy, since his clumsiness and pain had lowered his threshold for controlling himself.

The fog returned, but somewhere inside of it, he was able to work, as if the pain was also shrouded in a haze. If someone had asked him to describe exactly how he felt when the physical hardship began to push into his emotional response, he wouldn't have been able to put it into words.

But he often felt as if he was watching himself from the edge of a foggy lake, the steam rising up around this figure who was working hard and laboring under difficulty.

Only as Ginny brought him back down after a challenging work out did he feel the two sides of him come back together.

Sometimes he apologized for the way he acted, especially after his anger caused him to lash out with harsh words, but Ginny always laughed it off. "You're nothing compared to adolescent boys in a rage," she said. "Don't worry about me. I got this."

In the quieter moments, when he was at home with compresses on his legs or ice on aching parts, he realized Ginny was doing what the previous physical therapists had been unwilling to do. Whenever he had shown signs of breaking, when the PTSD started to rise up, they had backed off. This had meant he never moved as deeply into the rehabilitation as he'd needed.

He was grateful that she was sticking it out.

At Sunday dinner that week, he learned Melody had finished the renovation, and even cleaned up the back room. The windows had been scraped and the shelves were starting to fill. The aquarium installation was scheduled, and that was the point in which his mother felt she would need extra help. The tanks would require constant tending and supervision.

His father looked at him pointedly then, but he just mumbled that Melody could probably use the extra work and maybe she should stay on until school started.

Even his nephew, William, kept his distance. Between walking in a fog and this rumbling under the surface of his carefully controlled politeness, everyone knew he was on edge.

He could only hope that Ginny was right, and within a few weeks he would level out.

After dinner, his father took him aside in the backyard. "Son, I know you're going through some tough things right now. And I can't ever fully know everything."

Cody measured his breathing, trying not to lash out at the man who was just trying to say what he thought would help. But, no, his father would never know the places Cody had been, and the places he still had to go.

But instead of a lecture, his father passed him a hunk of wood and a small sharp knife.

"I always wondered if you had the family's skill," he said. "Grandpap had it, and my daddy had it, but it skipped me."

Cody turned over the wood. "Carving?" He'd always known his grandfather and great-grandfather had carved the small figures that resided over the fireplace, but his father had never done it or talked about it himself.

"Yeah. I don't think they did it so much to be crafty as give their hands something to do when their minds wouldn't be still."

Cody cut into the corner of the wood. It sliced neatly and cleanly, the shaving dropping to the dirt. A wave of satisfaction flowed through him at the neatness of the blade burying into the block.

"Basswood," his dad said. "Best wood for the job. Although there are others. It does take an eye for it. My dad always told me if you could see the finished sculpture, you could carve it. Unfortunately, I never could see anything but a hunk of wood."

Cody grunted. The wood was not a rectangular block, but uneven, and one of the small protrusions on the side reminded him of a dog's nose. He chipped away at that section until it looked like Tyrus's snout. He kept going, moving the knife around until he got a feel for how deep to make the cut and how the wood would chip away. Soon there were eyes and the rough outline of ears.

"I had a feeling," his dad said. "There are some online tutorials if you want to get into the nitty-gritty of how to go about it. But it looks like you got the eye and the touch."

"How come you never had me do this before?" Cody asked. He was already chipping away at the bottom to carve away the paws. The dog was sitting on his back haunches, he could see that clear as day in the wood. It was what the shape was always meant to be.

"You weren't ready for it then," he said. "My dad did tell me that. Not to try it too early, because if you gave up on it when you were young, you might never come back around to it."

Cody heard the words, but his thoughts were already whirring. Was the tail up or down? It was probably wrapped around his haunches. There really wasn't a section sticking out that would suggest an uplifted tail.

His father chuckled. "I'll leave you to it. I got a whole box of that wood in the garage, though, if you want it."

Cody nodded as his dad left, his mind still on the block. Tyrus lay down at his feet, and put his nose to the ground.

It seemed his dog wasn't worried about him at the moment either.

❦

For Melody, the next few weeks were a little on the lonely side.

Delivery people came in and out. Delilah popped in to check on her. The woman who arrived to install the fish tanks had been knowledgeable and fun and taught Melody all about aeration and pH balance and how tap water could kill.

But Melody definitely missed the days of working side-by-side with Cody. Whatever he was going through must be pretty serious because he hadn't even dropped by the bakery since the day he'd been so angry and upset.

The date was set for the Christmas in July Pet Parade, and Officer Stone sat down with her and Delilah so they could plan the parade route, the road closures, the timing of the event, and where the tables and booths would be set up on the Square.

In many ways, the weeks passed quickly, with lots of progress and excitement. Fred rustled up volunteers to help, and Melody recruited from her own pep squad so that plenty of townspeople would be around to direct both the spectators and the parade participants to the proper locations. The band director put together a decent-sized group of players to march along and play favorite tunes.

About two weeks before the parade, she popped into Maude and Gertrude's pie shop to ask if they would need electricity at their table.

Both of the women were sitting on stools behind the counter, looking typical for their personalities.

Maude was everyone's kindly grandmother in a crisp white apron, her tight black curls mixed with gray. Gertrude was a hot mess, her apron streaked with every type of pie filling, and sitting in a cloud of flour.

"What can we do for you?" Maude asked.

Gertrude spoke up before Melody could answer. "Looks like we could do her for at least three pieces of pie. She's skinny as a stick."

Classic Gertrude.

"I'm here to ask about your booth at the Christmas in July parade." Melody hopped onto one of the stools. "Do you need electricity? Are your pies going to need refrigeration?"

"We've got a special cooler for that," Maude said. "And I can always have a runner go back and forth between the shop and the booth if we need more."

Gertrude leaned forward on the counter and fixed her beady eyes on Melody. "You're not walking out this door until we put at least five hundred calories into you. So chocolate, apple, chess, or lemon meringue?"

Melody glanced at the case. "What's that red one?"

"Cherry and pear," Gertrude said. "That's what you want?"

"If you insist," Melody said, trying to hide her smirk.

"Oh, she does," Maude said. "It's her personal mission to make every lady in Applebottom as fluffy as her."

Gertrude whipped around. "Can it, Maude. Can't you see the girl's about to dry up and blow away? Tell me you don't want to feed that child."

Maude shook her head. "I'm quite sure our math teacher and pep squad coach can feed herself just fine."

Gertrude cut a huge chunk of pie and placed it on a plate. "Ice cream is not an option, vanilla or peach? Don't tell me chocolate. Chocolate doesn't go."

"Vanilla's fine," Melody said. She really was going to get five hundred calories.

"How are the plans for the parade coming?" Maude asked.

Melody flipped through her notebook and carefully wrote down that the pie booth did not need electricity.

"I've just got to get all the booths arranged so that we can get power to the ones that need it."

Gertrude plunked the pie plate in front of her. "Who needs power for a booth?"

"Janine wants to do massages for the pet owners. She insists she needs a fan."

"Diva," Gertrude said. "I'm thirty years older than her and I can handle a Missouri summer."

Melody picked up a fork and cut off a good-sized bite of pie.

But Gertrude wasn't done with her. "How come we haven't seen you and Cody walking around Town Square like you were a few weeks ago? We had the whole town planning your wedding."

Melody almost choked on her pie. "What?"

"Don't pay her any mind," Maude said. "They're all just a bunch of gossips."

"Like you weren't right in the middle of it," Gertrude said. "So what is it?"

"He's been off doing other things lately, so we haven't seen each other," Melody said.

Gertrude elbowed Maude. "See. I told you. That boy isn't sweet on anybody."

"Gertie, give it a rest. Can't you see you're upsetting her?"

Melody shrugged. "It's okay."

"Is he going to help with his mother's parade?" Gertrude asked.

"I honestly don't know," Melody said. "I hope so."

"Oh, she's got it bad," Gertrude said. She pointed a crooked finger at the back room. "Maude, go get his mother on the phone."

"I will do no such thing," Maude said. "We've dabbled enough in all this."

Melody wondered what they meant. There were definitely rumors, even in her circles, that the owners of the businesses on Town Square liked to pair up the single people in town. Some said they had forced Coach McBride to hang out with Ginny Page, who did occupational therapy at the high school on Fridays.

And others said they'd made Luke, the mayor's son, go help Savannah out at the animal shelter. And they were engaged now.

But nobody had forced Melody to go work in the bakery. That had been her idea.

"You just eat your pie, young lady," Maude said. "Don't worry about Gertie here. We'll keep her in check."

"Not if I see that boy at the parade," Gertrude said. "Ain't nobody in town who can make my gums stop flapping if I've got something to say."

"Ain't that the truth," said Maude.

They went on like this while Melody finished her pie. She didn't pop into the shop very often, not really having extra money to spend on sweets, but generally, this was their standard operating procedure.

She scraped the last bit of pie and ice cream off her plate and pushed it aside. "What do I owe you for the pie?" she asked.

Gertrude's hands went straight to her hips. "Girl, do not insult me. I am doing my civic duty to the starving young people of Applebottom."

Melody would've argued that she wasn't starving, but there was no point. Gertrude had her opinions, and she was going to say them. It had gotten her some free pie.

"Thank you," she said. "I need to move on and figure out the rest of these booths."

"You're doing a great job, honey," Maude called after her. "Don't let anybody tell you any different."

Melody picked up her notebook and headed back out onto the Square. It was midafternoon and blistering hot. She walked back to the bakery, admiring the clean shiny windows that now allowed the townspeople to see inside the pet store. She took stock in what she had done this summer so far.

She helped make this happen. She created a Christmas celebration that her grandmother was going to get to attend.

And maybe, if she were lucky, the man who interested her the most would return to her at the event that they had come up with together.

Who knew? Maybe even mean old Gertrude would do something that would help them out.

CHAPTER 18

*C*ody felt nerve-wracked the morning of the parade.

He'd been helping his mother from home, arranging for the trucks and trailers, as well as most of the motor cars that were involved.

His mom had handled the two nursing homes and worked with his dad to ensure that the trailers were safe and secure, covered, and outfitted with fans so the honored guests of the parade were comfortable.

The Applebottom home was sending seven residents, with four getting to reunite with their dogs for the day. Brookdale, where Melody's grandmother resided, was sending six people and two dogs, one of them being Mistletoe.

Technically, Cody's role was to wait in Town Square and direct people where to go once the parade concluded. But he had arranged for one of his high school buddies to manage that for him.

He was determined to walk in this parade, unaided.

He'd seen Melody only once since he left, about a week ago. He had weaned himself off the fog-inducing medication and discovered he was more or less in control again. His pain levels were higher than before he began renewed therapy, but then, he was trying harder. He'd done what Ginny had asked. He hadn't simply stuck to his strengths. He'd pushed his weaknesses.

He had no doubt that he was the best version of himself that he could be for the work he had done.

But talking to Melody, even for just a couple minutes, was like a smash to the heart. He wished that somehow he could have kept in contact with her throughout the whole ordeal. But that had been too risky.

He reached into his pocket and fingered a small woodcarving. It reminded him of what he was doing this for. Not really for Melody. But for his future. The hopes that he wanted to carry again. The light he once held but had lost.

He parked his Jeep, not behind the pet store as planned but at the staging area. One of the few questions he asked Melody the one time he'd seen her, looking bright and lovely next to the new aquariums in the store, was where she would be before the parade. She'd said in staging.

She hadn't appeared to be any different when speaking to him than she had in the weeks when they worked closely together. But Cody sensed that she was withholding something, some happy spark of herself.

He didn't blame her. He had snuffed out more than

one light during his journey to healing. He couldn't risk hers.

Cody arrived as the parade participants were beginning to assemble. His parents were already there, speaking to Officer Stone, who was assisting with the crowd control. Quite a few teen girls were setting out cones, and righting the clusters of small picket signs that had fallen over or pointed the wrong direction.

Cody stood watching from across the field. They were using an empty lot near the elementary school as a place to organize the participants. It would be a half-mile walk to Town Square.

His dad waved off from his mom and headed to his truck, which was parked just up the road from Cody's Jeep. He would likely be headed to the Square to supervise the booths.

His father spotted him and headed to the Jeep rather than his own truck. "Boy, what are you doing here? Aren't you stationed at the Square?"

Cody waited until his dad had stopped beside him to answer. "Simon is helping out in my place. I'm going to walk the parade."

His father glanced down at Tyrus sitting at their feet. "You run this by your mom?"

"Nope."

His dad pulled off his hat and wiped his hand over his mostly bald head, then replaced it. "You got some sort of plan?"

"Maybe." Cody fingered the carving again.

"I reckon you're a grown man," his dad said. "But you

might let your mother in on it so she doesn't have a freak-out. She's pretty high strung today."

"Advice noted."

His dad adjusted his hat again. "I reckon I better get on down there."

When his father had left, Cody stood another moment. Out of habit, he reached inside his car for his walking stick, then remembered he didn't want it.

Tyrus whined a bit when Cody closed the door without it. "It's all right, boy. It's all part of the plan."

He still walked with a pronounced limp, and his stride was more of a step-hop than the way most people put one foot in front of the other.

But he could do it. The question was how long, and how well, he'd hold up for a long distance. Didn't matter. He was doing it.

The sun bore down. Even at eight in the morning, sweat trickled down his back as he made his way up the street. Cody was just about to set out across the field when Archie pulled up in a steely blue 1957 Ford.

"What do you think of my choice as the parade marshal?" Archie asked, his football announcer voice very much in evidence, even in casual conversation.

"Love it," Cody said.

"You want a lift over to your mom? I'm apparently leading this pet parade."

Cody looked over the tall waving grass. It was a pretty long trek across the field and he could save his energy for the parade itself. Plus it kept the surprise.

He walked around to the passenger side. "Sure. I like arriving someplace in style." He settled onto the crisp vinyl seat and had Tyrus sit on the floorboard between his knees.

"Sorry for the lack of AC," Archie said. "Didn't exactly come standard back in the day."

Archie wore a jaunty gray Santa hat that matched the car. With his well-trimmed stark-white beard, he could almost pass for a hip Kris Kringle.

"Where's Matilda?" Cody asked. "I thought she'd be riding shotgun."

"My wife likes her creature comforts," he said. "Driving in July without air conditioning is not her idea of a good time."

They pulled up to where his mother stood with a clipboard. She leaned into the open window on Archie's side.

"Where do you want your star car?" Archie asked.

"Let me put the signs on you," his mom said. "Then you're going to pull right up to the corner so no one can get in front of you." She looked over at Cody. "Aren't you supposed to be at Town Square?"

"Good morning to you too, Mom," Cody said. "Simon's taking my place right now. I've got something to do over here."

"All right. It's not like this is the presidential inauguration or something." She stepped away from the car and gestured for a girl to come over with a big vinyl banner.

"Thanks for the ride," Cody said to Archie. "See you at the Square."

While the girl tied the banner to Archie's door handles, Cody stepped out. Time to show off.

His mother noticed right off. "Where's your cane?" she asked.

"Don't need it," he said.

Her mouth fell open, but then the banner slid off the Ford, and she leaped forward to help the girl with the nylon rope.

Good.

He scanned the crowd for Melody but didn't spot her. She said she'd be in staging. But there was no telling where. It was chaos, dogs and people and wagons everywhere, all trying to figure out what to do.

Two teen girls walked nearby and he waved them down, figuring they might be pep squad members. "Have you seen Melody?" he asked.

They giggled. "You mean Ms. Hopkins?"

"Right. Ms. Hopkins."

"She was headed to the nursing home tent last I saw her," one said, trying to straighten her jaunty red Santa hat, which kept slipping over her eyes.

Cody scanned the field. Near the road was a large green tent. A sign read, "Applebottom Nursing Home and Brookdale Residents Here."

Of course. Naturally, she'd be with her grandmother and organizing the honorees.

He hurried toward the tent. He'd discovered that the quicker he walked, the more normal his step-hop stride appeared. Tyrus trotted alongside him.

When he reached it, he opened the flap. Inside, a dozen elderly people and a few dogs sat surrounded by fans. A young woman passed out cups of lemonade.

But no Melody.

He was about to turn around again when a familiar *yip* caught his attention.

Mistletoe tore through the tent, dodging feet and wheelchairs, to stand beneath Tyrus.

Cody bent down to pet the little dog. "Where's Melody?" he asked.

But the dogs had no answers. Cody stood to leave when a tiny woman near the front said, "You must be Cody."

As soon as he looked into the woman's eyes, he knew this was Melody's grandmother. They had the same round shape and ocean blue.

"Come on," he said to the dogs and stepped into the tent properly. He kneeled next to the lady. "I am. And you are Grandma."

Her eyes twinkled the same way Melody's did, and a surge of affection rushed over him.

"Call me Layla," she said. "I hear you're a war veteran."

"Did a stint in Iraq," he said.

One of the men leaned forward in his chair. "I was in the Army, boy. Come sit next to me."

Grandma winked at him as the others peppered Cody with questions about his military duty, his service dog, and what he was doing now.

"I had PTSD coming out of 'Nam," one man said. "But we didn't know what it was then. They're just starting to get a real foothold on it now." He looked down at the dog. "This mutt helping you?"

"He does," Cody said. "He's a real smart one."

"Good, good," he said.

Officer Stone stepped into the room. "Ladies and gentlemen," he said. "It's time to load onto your trailer. I trust you will find it comfortable."

Two more girls appeared to take the cups from everyone and help with the move. The Vietnam vet asked Cody, "You think you can help me with this chair?"

"Certainly," he said.

Cody bent down and unlocked the wheels. One of the man's arms was in a sling, so Cody gripped the handle on the back to push.

"Come on, Tyrus. Come, Mistletoe," he said.

Layla stood beside him. "I think I'll just hang on to you," she said.

Whew, boy. He was in charge of a wheelchair, an elderly lady, and two dogs. And he was the invalid! But Cody just shot her a grin. "You do that."

They made their way out of the tent, down the short ramp off the curb, and into the line leading up to the trailer.

Several helpers came along, and one of them took the veteran off Cody's hands so they could lock him in place on the trailer. Cody helped Layla into a chair near the front and tied Mistletoe's leash to the chair.

"Are you going to ride with us?" Layla asked. "Melody will be along in a minute."

Cody hesitated. His whole goal was to walk this thing. That was the point of all the pain he'd been through. "I think I'll walk alongside."

But when all the residents were secure, the fans whirring, and more lemonade passed out again,

Mistletoe started howling as Cody and Tyrus started to leave.

"Poor little puppy dog," Layla said. "Maybe you could sit a spell until my granddaughter gets here."

That he could do. He dropped to the ground at Layla's feet, arranging the two dogs so they were out of everyone's way. There was only one chair left on the float, next to Layla and presumably for Melody. The other volunteers stationed themselves around the rows.

While he'd been talking to the residents, the entire parade had gotten into place. The field was mostly empty, just a few onlookers standing in the weeds. The cars were in the front, then the trailers with cheerleaders and a couple of other businesses. A tractor pulling hay bales held the official Santa Claus and a bunch of kids holding sacks of candy canes to toss.

Then their trailer.

Behind them the street was filled with people and pets, most of them dressed as Santa, elves, gingerbread men, or in various combinations of red, green, and gold.

"Look at that," Layla said. "It's a Christmas parade." Her eyes glistened. "I haven't been to one of these in years."

Cody reached up to pat her hand.

And that's when he spotted Melody.

Melody felt more than a little bit frantic.

They'd grossly underestimated the number of people who would ask for a number to be part of the costume contest. They only had one hundred and those had run out long ago.

Thankfully she'd had a huge reel of white poster paper in her trunk. Girls from her pep squad had been busily cutting squares off and manually writing new numbers with fat Sharpie markers.

The band director had rushed up, confused about the time, and was madly trying to organize the marchers between the cars and the trailers that were actually parked a little too closely for them to fit. They'd have to arrange their lines once the parade began.

Delilah was off the rails with anxiety. She was supposed to be in the back of the mayor's pick up truck by now, merrily opening bags so she could personally toss doggy and people treats out the back.

But instead, she was dashing up and down the parade lineup, checking in with everybody and stopping to pin numbers on some of the walkers.

The cacophony of barking drowned out everything.

The band director began warming up his contingent, adding random instrument noise to the insanity. Melody glanced at her watch. It was already five minutes until step-off.

Sarah, one of her pep squad girls, ran up to her. "We have everyone pinned. The list is a bit messy since I had to squeeze all the names in, but we should be able to figure out the winners when the judges give us numbers."

Melody let out a sigh. "Good job, Sarah. Really. Thank you."

Her friend Sybil caught up to them. "Where should we go?"

"Walk among the dogs and help anyone who gets in trouble," Melody said. "When we get to the Square, you can move everyone to the booths."

"Okay!" Sarah said. "Oh, and some man was looking for you!" The girl's eyes got all bright. "He was cute!"

No telling who that was. Cody was far away at the Square. "I'm sure he'll find me again," Melody said.

The two girls ran off to the walking section.

Delilah finally climbed into the back of the truck. Everything seemed to be in place. Melody could only assume all was well on the other end of the route where the booths would be waiting, as well as the spectators.

A whistle blew, and the band started a cadence. A great cheer went up from the crowd and Officer Stone's lights started flashing on his squad car at the back.

It was time. She needed to catch up to the nursing home trailer!

As she hustled along, she really took in what they had done. Dogs dressed as elves. People as Santa. Jingle bells and light-up hats. Everyone said, "Ho, ho, ho!" and "Merry Christmas in July!" as she passed.

They had done it.

The cars started moving forward. Eek. She had to catch up! She broke into a light run.

When she approached the trailer, one of the volunteers called, "Stop and let Melody on!"

A chorus of "Stop!" rippled across the trailer, but between the marching band and the dogs, there was no way the driver could hear.

Melody ran alongside the trailer a moment, glad she was in decent shape. The faces of the residents were a blur as she trundled along.

Then they reached the stop sign at the end of the street and the truck pulling the trailer came to a halt.

"Jump on!" several people called.

Melody put her foot up on the back, looking for somewhere to grab hold, when a strong, familiar hand reached out for her.

She looked up.

It was Cody.

🐾

Cody didn't know what he expected when her gaze met his. He was acutely aware of his wild hair, whipped by the fan blowing too close to his head.

But she smiled at him as he pulled her up onto the trailer.

Layla started clapping when Melody stood among the chairs, and the other people on the trailer joined in. She gave a little bow.

The trailer shifted forward, and she plopped down into the empty chair.

Cody sat on the floor by the dogs, anticipation thrumming through him now that he was in her presence again.

Her green outfit that seemed rather nondescript as he had pulled her up proved to be an elf costume. Short-sleeved, with shorts, and a little red kerchief tucked in the front pocket.

She wore pointy green felt covers with jingle bells over her tennis shoes.

Layla looked at the two of them expectantly. "So…"

"Oh!" Melody said. "Grandma, this is Cody."

"I know that," she said. "I've been talking to him for half an hour. I mean, why aren't you two talking?"

Cody swallowed, hoping his dry throat would work. All he could think to say was, "Where's your elf hat?"

Melody reached behind her and pulled a long green hat from her back pocket and stuck it on her head. "I like your shirt."

He glanced down. He wore a red T-shirt with a giant face of the Grinch filling the entire space. It read, "Where's the roast beast?"

"It's about as festive as I can get in this heat."

They sat there for a moment, just looking at each other.

Layla cleared her throat and looked between them expectantly.

Melody went first. "I missed having you around."

His heart hit the floor. Had she? Had he done the right thing by leaving?

"I missed you, too," he said.

He glanced at Layla, who seemed pleased with this. Obviously, Melody had told her everything.

"Oh, I have something. I made it." Cody pulled the carving from his pocket and passed it to Melody.

"It's Mistletoe! In a Santa hat!" Melody examined it carefully.

"Something to remember this day by," he said.

"I love it!" She clutched it and her happy expression made him warm all over again.

"What a nice surprise," Layla said. Her grin was as wide as theirs.

Cody washed over with relief. He had to believe leaving her for a while was necessary. He wanted to work hard, to push himself, and that wasn't something to do around someone as beautiful and bright as Melody. It took a professional like Ginny to handle him.

But he was better. It would be better now.

"I'm glad you got moved over here this morning rather than the Square," she said.

"Well, a sort of emancipated myself. My friend Simon took my shift," he said.

"I'm sure we'll need all the help we can get," she said.

"I wanted to be here with you," he rushed out.

She tilted her head. "I figured you couldn't live without me for long."

His heart thundered in his chest. "You know me that well?"

"I think I do."

Now Layla's smile was huge.

The trailer turned another corner and, suddenly, the crowd noise burst through. Throngs of townspeople stood along the walk, waving and cheering as they passed. Some wore Santa hats. Others went full Christmas in red and green, some in ugly holiday sweaters, even in the heat.

"Well, isn't this just splendid," Layla said. "You all really know how to do Christmas in July."

"Didn't think I'd be celebrating this holiday again,"

one of the men said. "I'm stage four and just turned down treatment."

Melody reached out and held the man's hand. "I'm glad you're here."

"I just love Christmas," Layla said.

"Don't we all?" Melody asked.

The band began to play *We Wish You a Merry Christmas* and one of the old ladies on the trailer started singing. The others joined in, and soon the raucous sound of the carolers drowned out the barking of the dogs.

Cody looked over at Melody. He wasn't a singer, generally, but when she shrugged and joined in, he decided, yeah, time to turn over an entirely new leaf.

So he sang along.

They reached the Square all too quickly. Cody wished the parade were miles long. He'd been ready to walk it, but this had worked out so well. And he could have done it either way, he realized. He didn't have to change to have a good time.

He was doing just fine as he was.

The band took a break as they approached the judges' station. The three women there stood up with their clipboards, trying to see the dogs. Behind the trailer, the crowd of walkers slowed down, all trying to get close to the table to show off their costumes.

"Look at that one," Layla said, pointing at a Santa with at least six leashes and leading matching brown Chihuahuas with red noses and antlers.

"Too cute!" Melody said. "Somewhere there's a

wagon made into a sleigh." She stood up. "See it, halfway back?"

"How adorable," Layla said.

Cody enjoyed watching them more than the entrants. Their delighted faces and astonished gasps at some of the more elaborate costumes was enough to make anyone smile.

The trailer slowed down and rolled to a stop. Everyone looked around, wondering what was the matter, but then the band struck up another carol and nobody cared anymore.

They sang *Frosty the Snowman* and *Rudolph*, and the volunteers passed out more lemonade. It was cool and pleasant with the fans blowing directly on them, the tent top blocking the sun. Cody could have stayed there all day.

But eventually, they lurched forward. As the parade progressed into the Square, Cody saw the holdup. There were hundreds of people, maybe over a thousand, crowding along the sidewalks.

"Whoa," Melody said. "I had no idea this was going to happen."

"You outdid yourselves," Layla said.

"Mom's going to freak," Cody said. "I should jump out to help."

"Me too." Melody gave her Grandma a kiss. "I'll find you in the special tent we have set up for you all."

"Aren't we spoiled?" Layla said.

When the trailer was forced to stop again, Melody walked to the back and jumped off.

"What should we do with the dogs?" Cody asked her.

"I've got 'em!" Layla said. "They sure are sweet on each other!"

Tyrus stood up in concern as Cody shifted to the end of the trailer.

"Tyrus, stay," he said.

One of the volunteers moved forward. "I'll handle them," she said.

"Thank you, Rita," Melody said. "Just put them in the tent."

Cody slid off the end and hopped down. As he expected, his tendons had tightened up from sitting on the floor. He bounced on the balls of his feet, trying to warm them again.

"Where's your stick?" Melody asked.

Instead of answering, Cody held out his hand to take hers. She looked at him in surprise, and for a moment fear shot through him that she'd turn him down.

But she smiled and grasped it.

And together they walked, or, she walked and he step-hopped, into the chaos of Town Square.

CHAPTER 19

*M*elody now had an idea why Cody had been gone for a while, and why he'd been in so much pain that one day.

He'd been doing something to help his leg.

She realized the faster they walked, the easier it was on him, so they hurried across the street to the center of the Square.

Delilah had already abandoned the mayor's truck and stood in the chaos, looking frantic.

"There are so many people!" she cried when she saw them. "And the walkers aren't even here yet!"

Maude stepped out from behind her table. "Don't you fret, Delilah. We've got enough pie to feed an army."

"But our cute dog-head cookies. I won't have enough. Half the people won't even see my business name." Delilah swiped at her eyes.

"Go to your bakery," Maude said. "Defrost everything in your freezer. It's going to be fine."

Cody stepped forward to give her a quick hug. "I'll take everything out. You're going to make a killing."

Delilah drew in a big breath. "You think it will be okay?"

"It will be more than okay," he assured her. "It will be spectacular."

He and Melody hurried to the far end of the Square, where the bakery and pet store were opened wide and staffed with volunteers who were showing off the space.

Quite a few people were inside, including Cody's sister Helen. Melody had met her several times in the course of setting up the pet store.

"We're going to sell out of literally everything," Helen said. She handed a woman change and turned to the next customer.

They approached the side counter. "Mom said to defrost everything," Cody said. "I'll bring you more and take the rest for the booth."

"I can't believe she threw hundreds of packages off a truck when we have such a crowd."

"It's all good. Everybody's happy."

Helen smiled at another customer and began filling a bag with dog biscuits, but her gaze just briefly touched on Melody and Cody's joined hands.

Melody felt a little zip go through her. Everyone would see. Would know!

"Let's go," Cody said, pulling her through to the back room.

"I feel like we're doing some covert op," Melody said.

"Trust me, the real thing is nothing like this."

She'd made another gaffe. Of course, them running

through a bakery to get dog cookies was nothing like a military mission.

But then he said, "Mess kits don't have fresh cookies."

Melody burst out laughing as he pulled her into a giant cooler filled with meat and supplies.

The cool air was a relief after all the heat and pressure and madness outside. For the first time, Melody felt she could take a breath.

"This has been nuts," she said.

"It has." He paused beside her, their hands still joined.

The cooler was narrow, cool, and dim compared to the outdoors. Melody could feel her heart hammering against her ribs. They were alone.

"We make a pretty good team," Cody said. His eyes glittered in the low light.

"We do," she said, feeling breathless all over again. He was so close, his hair tufting around his head, his gaze on her.

"I'm sorry I had to leave so abruptly," he said.

"It's okay—"

"No, I should have explained. I just...I just wasn't sure it was going to work out."

"What? Us?"

He squeezed her hand. "No! The therapy. I went back in for my leg. I wanted..." He trailed off.

"To walk without the cane?" she ventured.

"I wanted to feel normal again. Like an ordinary person."

She bit her lip. There would be no lightening this

conversion, no silly quips. She had to play it straight. "Well, I always felt the stick was very distinguished. And I think normal is highly overrated. Ordinary, too. I was just fine with Cody Jones the way he came."

"So Cody 2.0 wasn't necessary?"

"No. But I sort of like the way he turned out." She lifted her face to his. "Mostly."

"Mostly?"

"I'd like him better if I could get him out of Apple-bottom for a day."

"You mean like a date?"

"Yes."

"You're asking me out?"

"Sometimes a girl has to help a clueless boy out."

He grinned down at her, and her heart nearly swooped out if her chest. His eyes moved to the door, then back to her.

Then he leaned in.

When their lips met, Melody felt her entire body light up. Forget Christmas in July, this was Independence Day, fireworks and sizzle and colors in the sky.

His hands moved through her hair, knocking her elf hat askew. She tucked herself in close, feeling the warmth of him against her.

This is what she'd waited for. This is what she'd always wanted.

And now she'd never give it up.

When Helen knocked on the door of the cooler, Melody

quickly snatched up a container full of bone-shaped biscuits.

"Here," she said, quickly handing the plastic bin to Cody, and opened the door.

Helen accepted the bin, lifting an eyebrow as if to question what the two of them had been up to in there.

"I'll take this one," Melody said, picking up another one. "Let's package them as fast as we can."

"Riiight," Helen said, but she left them alone.

Cody laughed as he led Melody out of the cooler. They dropped their bins on a cabinet in the back, and he yanked open drawers. They hurriedly unloaded packages of cellophane bags.

"It will take too long to tie them," Melody said. "Let's close them up with her logo stickers. Kill two birds with one stone."

"Good thinking."

They rapidly filled dozens and dozens of bags and stickered them closed.

"These look great," Melody said. They threw them in a box. Most were already half defrosted.

The bakery had quieted some, and Helen leaned against the counter. "Got some ready?" she asked.

"We're running them out to Mom now."

"Good luck. Let me have a few for people who don't want a custom order." Helen took a handful of prepackaged biscuits and dropped them into the baskets sitting along the counter.

"Let's go," Cody said. They rushed back out into the heat of midday.

"Hey," Melody said. She stood still on a quiet part of the sidewalk.

He turned and looked back at her. Once again, her heart turned over in her chest.

"Are we going to let everybody know what's up?" she asked.

He shifted the box to one arm and held out his arm.

"We certainly are."

They clasped hands and hurried out together into the beautiful July day, surrounded by everyone they knew and loved, the whole darn town.

And nobody was surprised to see them at all.

CHAPTER 20

*B*oth Tyrus and Mistletoe sat at Cody's feet as Melody stopped by the front desk to let them know she was headed back to find her grandmother.

As the woman checked to make sure that Grandma was in her room and not off at a therapy, Melody glanced over at the little trio. Both the dogs wore their sharp *Service Dog* vests.

It had taken months to get Mistletoe in proper shape to pass her therapy dog training, but thankfully the bar for that sort of dog was a bit lower than service dogs like Tyrus, who had a more critical function with their owners.

It was enough to get her inside the facility, with the bonus that the Pomeranian was now better mannered and less likely to run wildly snapping at other dogs when she felt threatened.

Even so, only official service dogs that were part of the staff initiatives were eligible to go back into the patient rooms. But Melody didn't mind meeting in the spacious living area, especially today, with a Christmas celebration about to begin.

The room had beautiful, soft sofas and a piano in the corner. When they were lucky, Martin, one of the residents, would come out and play holiday carols. He would be starting any minute for the party.

"She's in her room," the woman at the desk said.

"Thank you."

Grandma had finished the rounds of chemotherapy that was causing the sun sensitivity. While the cancer had not been eradicated, the treatment definitely slowed it down and put more time on the board.

Melody would accept anything she got. She didn't kid herself that her grandmother would be around forever, but there would be one more real December 25th Christmas together.

This one would also be with Cody.

"Can you watch them for a minute?" Melody asked. "I'm going to run down to her room."

"Not a problem," Cody said. "I'll take them to the sofas." He reached down and scratched both of the dogs on their heads.

As Melody hurried past the front desk and through the labyrinth of hallways to her grandmother's room, she couldn't help but smile to herself.

She wouldn't call the last six months magical, exactly. But they had been good.

The summer had proven crazy with the opening of the pet store. Cody and Melody had worked there together in the busiest first weeks, their dogs happily snuggled together in a corner.

When school started, Melody returned to her position as math teacher and pep squad coach. And because it was fall, that meant a lot of football games and pep rallies and poster painting. She saw Cody less, but their time together became more pointedly about each other. They went on official dates, and there was no longer any doubt they were a couple.

For now, Cody was content to work in his mother's pet shop. But he had bigger plans. He'd already started working with a company who wanted to build a better hardware and phone app combination for people with PTSD, including kids.

He got permission to work with some of Ginny's students, and all the technology and electronic expertise he'd picked up in the service laid the foundation for the continuing education classes. He was taking online to fill in his gaps to become more proficient at both sides of the development.

Melody didn't know if this work would eventually take him away from Applebottom, but she might be okay if it did, as long as they got to be together. Math teachers, particularly female math teachers, were something she'd learned was in short supply. She felt confident she could work anywhere, from a big city to a tiny town.

Her grandmother's door was closed, so she knocked on it.

"Just a moment," her grandmother called. "Getting prettied up!"

After a minute, the door opened, and one of the kindly staff members at Brookdale smiled at her. "She wanted to get her hair perfect," the woman said. "You'll help her down?"

"I will," Melody said.

The woman opened the door wide, and Melody's eyes sparked seeing her grandmother standing by one of the chairs in her room.

She wore a silvery dress and a bright red poinsettia pinned in her puffy gray hair.

Grandma turned her head so that Melody could admire it. "What do you think? Am I too old for a flower in my hair?"

"You're never too old for that."

Grandma took hold of Melody's arm, and they walked carefully down the hall and back to the great room. Despite having slowed her cancer down again, Grandma was weaker than before the chemotherapy. But she was still walking, and she was here. She still had good days. Sometimes that was all anyone could ask for.

"You still driving up to see your mom after this?" Grandma asked.

"We are, dogs and all."

"Is Cody ready to meet her?"

"I think so. She's not so scary."

"I look forward to seeing her in a few days."

"I wish you'd drive up with us."

Grandma patted her arm. "I know my limits, my love. And four hours in a car isn't something that would suit me well."

"Well, I'll come up again when Mom is here. I have two weeks off."

"That will be lovely."

The music filtered into the hall as they approached the desk, passing through to the great room. Dozens of residents had assembled, and Martin merrily played *Good King Wenceslaus* on the piano. A few people were gamely trying to sing, but only a few actually knew the words.

Grandma sat on the sofa next to Cody and the dogs.

"How are all the puppies?" she asked. She fumbled in her purse and pulled out two dog biscuits. "A little Christmas treat!"

Mistletoe snapped hers greedily, but Tyrus politely waited until Grandma's hand was in the right spot before carefully licking it from her palm.

"Such a good dog," she said.

Leo, the Vietnam veteran Cody had gotten to know at the Christmas in July parade, had one of the staff members push him closer to their spot. "Merry Christmas!" he said. "Who knew we'd still be kicking in December."

"Tell me about it," Grandma said. "Maybe there's a little spark in the old bones after all."

Melody caught Cody's gaze and they smiled. This sort of exchange was the norm inside the facility.

Martin began playing *I'll Be Home for Christmas* and many of the residents chimed in. Quite a few had tears in their eyes, no doubt thinking of those loved ones who weren't with them this year.

Melody held her grandma's hand a little tighter. She

wouldn't take this Christmas for granted. Not any one of them. And come July, if Grandma was still able to get up and around, she knew she'd be celebrating Christmas in July all over again.

And, this time, there was no doubt who all would be by her side.

EPILOGUE

*C*hristmas came around pretty often these days.

Cody strung a set of twinkling lights through the trees on the circular path behind the Brookdale retirement home. Twilight would begin to descend soon, and he needed to finish the job.

It was March, and Melody was on spring break. With all the friends they had gotten to know at the facility, it made sense to come more often, and today, to have a little more Christmas.

Cody teetered on the stepladder, and Tyrus gave out a sharp warning bark.

"I've got it, don't worry," he told his dog.

Tyrus's bark was rare, so Mistletoe ran in tight little circles, filled with anxiety.

"Mistletoe, calm down. I'm fine." What a pair of worrywarts they were.

Melody rushed out the back door with a box of ornaments. "Some of these are fresh off the hot glue gun," she said.

"Did everybody get one done?"

"They did. Maria has been going crazy trying to make sure everyone could participate."

The decision to have Christmas in March, as well as July and the traditional December, had been made when Leo, the veteran they had befriended, had a stroke.

He could still sit in his wheelchair, and although he didn't speak anymore, Cody could usually figure out what the old man was trying to say.

And when he'd managed to drag an old line of tinsel from his room into the living area a few weeks ago, Cody knew exactly what he was after.

"Do you think there will be enough light?" Melody asked.

"I'll string up two more," Cody said. "We have a ton."

Melody nodded and hurried back toward the doors. "I'll get Grandma ready."

They didn't have a Christmas tree exactly, but a tall bush, reaching well above Cody's head, had roughly the right shape. Once strung with lights and filled with ornaments, it definitely passed.

Cody added two more strings to the crisscross between the trees and stood back to look at his work. He was pretty sure they had enough lights up now. He picked up the box Melody had left and added the last collection of ornaments to the Christmas bush.

For the first time since he had started preparing the back yard for the Christmas celebration, Cody felt a wave of nervousness. This was a bigger night than any of them knew. And he had to pull it off just right.

LaFonda, one of the senior staff members, came out

to look over his work. "This looks great, Cody," she said. The light glinted off her glossy black braids and glittered in her warm brown eyes. "They are going to love this. I agree that a quarterly Christmas is something we should consider."

"They do seem to like it," Cody said. "I'm not sure you would want to do it every day, but every three months seems like a good distance."

"They're going to bring the sound system out next," she said. "Melody said you had a playlist?"

"I do," he said. "I'll just connect my phone to it and it'll play."

"Sounds like everything is together. We have the staff setting up drinks and cookies in the rec room. So we will come out here and sing a few carols, and then we'll go in for refreshments."

"Perfect plan."

A young man walked out with a large speaker on wheels. "Here's the sound," he said.

"Thanks," Cody said. The two of them worked a moment to connect his phone and the first song began to play *It's Beginning to Look a Lot Like Christmas.*

Several of the residents wandered out at the sound, finding a bench or a chair to sit on and admire the lights.

By the time the music switched to *Let It Snow*, a good number of people were outside.

The evening was chilly, but not bitterly cold. A few attendants rushed inside and returned with light blankets to put around the residents who hadn't worn coats. Cody watched for Melody to return with her grandmother, a light sweat breaking out on the back of his neck despite the chill.

He needed her to be out here by song four or he would have to alter his plan.

As the third song queued up, everyone began to sing *Jingle Bells*. He was about ready to rearrange his entire playlist when Melody finally emerged with her grandmother.

Layla preferred to walk under her own power, but she used a walker to steady herself these days. The two of them arrived at the chairs, and Melody settled her grandmother on one and perched next to her on another. The two dogs abandoned Cody and sat at the women's feet.

Since the singing was going well, Cody did actually rearrange the playlist, letting *Deck the Halls* and *We Wish You a Merry Christmas* play while everyone sang before the speaker went oddly quiet.

The young man monitoring the sound system gave him a nod and handed him a microphone.

"Hey everybody," Cody said. His voice reverberated throughout the circle, catching everyone's attention. "Merry Christmas."

Everyone laughed and repeated, "Merry Christmas," back to him.

"Nothing like Christmas in March. Who needs St. Patrick's Day when you can have Saint Nick?"

More laughter.

"I'm very pleased to be part of this new tradition here at Brookdale. Tonight's Christmas was the brainchild of our friend Leo Schmidt, who also feels like you can never have too much Christmas."

Cody gestured to Leo, who managed to nod his head and give a half-smile. Applause broke out across the circle.

"I have to admit, though, that I had a bit more personal of a reason to want to put on this Christmas in March." He hesitated, realizing Melody had looked up from her grandmother curiously to see what he had to say.

"Melody, would you come up here?"

He knew Melody was not shy in front of crowds. It came with being the pep squad coach and a teacher. But she hesitated, and only when her grandmother patted her on the arm and gestured for her to move forward did she actually get out of the chair.

Cody drew in a steadying breath. When he was a young man, he hadn't given much thought to what his marriage proposal would look like. He'd seen tons of YouTube videos. Crazy things like huge dance numbers. Having a marquee lit up with the question. Skywriting. He particularly remembered one where an entire movie theater had been taken over, with the lead up to the proposal being a man running into the seats with a ring.

Certainly, during his darkest days as he was going through his recovery, thinking his life had been destroyed by that AED in Iraq, he hadn't pictured a proposal to anyone at all.

But now, here she was. He was pretty sure what her answer would be, so that didn't cause him any nervousness at all.

It was just the idea of taking this step. Of doing the thing that he thought was lost to him, but had somehow been miraculously returned.

Melody petted the dogs before walking up to the front. Her red dress sparkled with glittery shine, like the ornaments the residents had made.

So many people had helped him on this journey to her. Most of them he would never see again. Nurses and doctors and therapists from the VA hospital.

Certainly Ginny, who knew that this was happening today. And his parents, who were actually probably hiding somewhere in the bushes because they also knew this moment was occurring.

But most of all, it was Melody herself.

And now she stood next to him.

"What's going on?" she asked.

He answered by saying, "Melody Hopkins, you are the best thing that's ever happened to me."

He no more got the words out when Melody's eyes sparkled brightly with tears.

So she knew. Of course she did. She did teach calculus, after all. She was the smartest person he'd ever met.

He had practiced the next move a hundred times to make sure he could do it smoothly without falling over and embarrassing himself.

He got down on one knee. His good knee, of course, because he wasn't crazy.

The residents circling them in the twinkling lights gave a collective sigh.

Tyrus got up and padded over to them, sitting at his

side. Mistletoe, not to be abandoned, trotted up next to fill out their quartet.

The gang was all there.

Cody cleared his throat. "Ever since I met you, I have been driven to become a better man. For a long time, I thought that meant I had to change what damaged me. That I had to be closer to the person I was before."

Melody bit her lip and reached down to take his hand. He felt stronger with that connection between them.

"What you taught me was that sometimes acceptance is more important than change. That even if I was not who I used to be, I could be someone better. Because of this, I know you are the perfect person to walk beside me on this journey through my life. So I ask you, Melody Hopkins, will you do that? Will you be my wife?"

Melody only nodded at first, as if she couldn't trust her voice. Then she said, "Yes." Her voice broke, but she got it back. "Yes, Cody. I will marry you."

The entire back patio of Brookdale broke into cheers and claps and happy shouts.

He spotted Layla wiping her eyes and realized quite a number of the residents were doing the same.

There was nothing like love to make everyone remember all the amazing things they had experienced in their lifetimes. They were surrounded by evidence of it; men and women who had lived full lives, and hoped for a little more of that happiness before their time was complete.

And nothing better was the kind of joy you felt at Christmas. Especially when you were witnessing love.

He slipped the ring on Melody's finger, and when he seemed to struggle to stand up, she reached down to hug him, and together he got back to his feet.

That's where true love came from. Not in expecting perfection in each other. But in helping each other to be the best they could be.

And in that, he and Melody were a perfect fit.

I'm so happy for Melody and Cody (and Mistletoe and Tyrus!)

Don't miss their wedding! It's a bonus epilogue for email and text subscribers.

Sign up on her web site for emails.

Or text ABBYT to 77948 (US only) for text!

Love Applebottom?
See some of the characters you met here again:

Ginny, who helped Cody with his renewed therapy, is the main character in *The Perfect Disaster*, where her oversized Great Dane requires help from the local football coach at Applebottom High.

Sandy, who decorated the amazing dog cookies that Cody gave to Melody, is the main character in *The Sweetest Match*, where the town discovers she's hiding secret words of love and longing on the cakes she decorates for Betty at Tea for Two.

Fred Jones, Delilah's husband, is the fire chief who shows up when Betty's granddaughter Lorelei sets the lawn on fire, attracting local firefighter Micah in *The Irresistible Spark*.

Gertrude writes ALL the meeting minutes at the beginning of every Applebottom book, and she also narrates the weddings of all the Applebottom couples, which are bonus epilogues sent to newsletter and text subscribers. (Hint: There might be something getting started between Gertrude and Alfred Felmont in the epilogues only!) Make sure you get those, as she's a HOOT! www.abbytyler.com/news.

GERTRUDE & MAUDE'S
STRAWBERRY RHUBARB PIE

CRUST

• Any top and bottom pastry crust. Store bought is fine, if you want to be lazy like that.
(Gertie, you can't be rude to people if you're not going to cough up your own pastry crust recipe.)
(*Maude, what's the point of getting old if you can't be rude?*)

FILLING

• 2 1/2 cups rhubarb (2-3 stalks cut up, but frozen is just fine too)
(*Says you, Maude. I like it fresh.*)
(How was the pie this morning, Gertie?)
(*Just fine. Could have used a touch more zest.*)
(Well, that was 2/3 of a bag from the frozen food aisle.)
(*What?*)

(Yes, I put frozen rhubarb in the pie.)
(*Are you trying to pick a fight with me, Maude?*)
(You say that like it's hard.)

- **2 pints cut-up strawberries**

- **1 cup sugar**

- **1 small container vanilla yogurt**

- **a lemon for zest**

- **2 tablespoons flour**

- **1 tablespoon butter, cut into bits**

INSTRUCTIONS

1. Preheat the oven to 375°F.
2. For the crust: Lay the bottom crust into the pie pan. Place a half-dozen small cuts in the bottom so it will cook evenly.
3. For the filling: Slice the strawberries and cut the rhubarb into 1/2 inch chunks, discarding the ends.
4. Sprinkle the sugar over the fruit and turn it until it's evenly coated.
5. Give the lemon a few good scrapes with the zester and turn it all again. (*Make sure there are several good zests, unless you want a boring ol' pie*

like Maude with her fraudulent rhubarb.) (Fraudulent rhubarb? Does that make you fraudulent Gertrude since you're just as frosty as that frozen veggie?) *(I thought we weren't going to admit that rhubarb is a vegetable.)* (You can't lie about what it is, Gertie.) *(Well, now they won't make it.)* (Sure they will.) *(And why is that? Who wants vegetable pie for dessert?)* (Because it's our recipe, and we're the best.) *(Well, I'll give you that.)*

6. Dump the container of vanilla yogurt into the fruit and mix. *(You've given away our secret ingredient, Maude.)* (I know it.) *(How are we going to keep our pie customers if they can make it themselves?)* (We can't keep all the secrets, Gertie. We're going to die one day.) *(Well, aren't you bright and cheerful?)* (They'll still buy our pies, Gertie, don't you worry.)

7. Spread the filling onto the crust in the pie plate.

8. Sprinkle the flour over the filling to help thicken the liquid. Dot with butter.

9. Layer the top crust over the pie, cutting slits for ventilation. For our pie, we like to do a circle lattice, but you can top it any old way. We brush the top of the pie with egg whites and sprinkle a bit more sugar over it before baking, but that's optional. *(You going to tell them how to make the circle lattice?)* (Oh, sure. Take two sizes of biscuit cutters, or two sizes of drinking glasses, and cut circles in the

dough. Layer the outside lines of the circles and the inner circles however looks pretty to you.) *(You got pictures, because that was clear as mud, Maude.)* (I have pictures.)

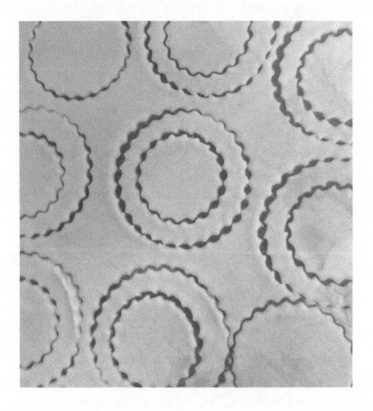

Bake the pie at 375 degrees for 20 minutes, then cover the edges of the pie to avoid burning. Bake an additional 20 minutes. Depending on how you decorated your crust, you may need to bake it slightly longer or shorter to avoid over browning.

Enjoy your pie and don't miss more of Gertrude and Maude in the other Applebottom books!

ABOUT ABBY TYLER

Abby Tyler loves puppy dogs, pie, and small towns (she grew up in one!) Her Applebottom Matchmaker Society books combine the sweet and wholesome style of romance she loves with the funny, sometimes a-little-too-truthful characters she remembers from growing up in a place where everyone knew everybody's business.

Join her mail or text list for a bonus epilogue for every book, a wedding scene narrated by Gertrude!

The Applebottom Matchmaker Society books include:

- *The Sweetest Match*
- *The Perfect Disaster*

- *The Irresistible Spark*
- *The Unexpected Shelter*
- *Mistletoe Summer*
- *The Special Delivery*

with many more planned!

facebook.com/authorabbytyler

twitter.com/abbytylerauthor

instagram.com/abbytylerauthor

bookbub.com/authors/abby-tyler

CPSIA information can be obtained
at www.ICGtesting.com
Printed in the USA
LVHW091332160720
660862LV00002B/559

9 781938 150890